The Future In the Sky

The Empyrean Saga Book One

Steve Stred

BVP

Black Void Publishing

Contents

The Empyrean Saga Series

The Empyrean Saga Series
  Book 1: The Future In the Sky
  Book 2: The Bandaged
  Book 3: The Devourers
  Book 4: The Returned
  Book 5: Where All Light Ends
  Book 6: An Orange Sky Shines Down (The Empyrean Saga Poetry Companion)

Advance Praise For The Future In the Sky

Advance Praise for *The Future In the Sky*

"In an overpopulated ship revolving above Earth, teens must leap for Salvation. But what exactly does that mean? In *The Future In the Sky*, a mind-bending post-apocalyptic study of survival, betrayal, and revenge, Stred solidifies his place as a creator of fresh nightmares. Take a leap of faith and read this book."

- Lee Murray, three-time HWA Bram Stoker Award - nominee and author of *Into the Ashes*.

"Dark science fiction with a compulsively readable writing style and a strong emotional core."

- Tim Waggoner, HWA Bram Stoker Award-Winning author and author of *Your Turn to Suffer*.

0. Start

The students stared beyond the window, toward the infinite.

The all-consuming darkness of space. An everlasting void. A longing to know what was to come. The weightless feeling of complete bliss. The all-encompassing light of the future. A decision would be announced soon, the ones making it enroute.

Rolling clouds.

Heart shaped hands.

Sweet laughter of innocence swept along the current of anxiety.

The playgrounds no longer just forgotten structures. Running, jumping, shouting, play time. What was ahead was pushing what came before away. A sorrow of the truth flickered here and there, but some would continue, others not so lucky.

Childish rhymes of sing-song play echoed all around as the world they knew rotated around its axis. The mix of ages was an interesting dance to watch. The youth cavorting, the older, high school aged kids sitting on the periphery.

The Earth 250,000 miles below, the atmosphere thinned and speckled.

What would be found below the foliage? How would the air taste and the breeze dance?

A bell sounded to tell them all to return to their classrooms.

1. Decision

The door to the classroom opened. Their teacher, Mr. Haverstock, entered, followed by two people the students didn't recognize. Worried glances between them all shared their fears.

"Quiet, please. Quiet. Attention class. We have a very important announcement. Please select digital imprint on your retinal screens now."

*

An old time countdown begins before the students' eyes. Some take notice, others remain slumped in their desks, absent of caring.

The reel flickers before the black and white scene begins. First, they see a tall, thin man in a grey suit, sporting a bushy moustache and sitting on the edge of a desk, inspecting a file folder.

He looks up, mock surprise at the camera nearby, and speaks.

'Ah, children. Hello. My name is Albert Eldridge. I am the owner, founder, and chief scientist of Empyrean...'

When the students hear the name, they all cheer, ignoring the teacher's and administrators' pleas to remain calm. Once they've settled, the digital administrator moves the imprint back to where they lost control.

'... and you've been selected as my next class to have your life's dreams fulfilled. You see, here at Empyrean, we look into the future to bring the present to you. Buckle up, my star pupils. The next three years will be like nothing you've ever experienced before.

The large 'E' logo of Empyrean with the soaring eagle and spaceship comes onto the imprint, then all goes black.

*

"That's right, students. Of the seventy-five classes that submitted for Survival and Salvation, our class was chosen by Albert Eldridge himself," Mr. Haverstock said, grin across his face. He turned and shook hands with the two administrators, who unzipped their black jackets to reveal Empyrean emblazoned shirts underneath.

Throughout the revolving level, beyond the walls of the classroom, screams and bangs sounded, the Empyrean squad eradicating the classes that weren't picked.

Only the chosen would carry on, continue the tradition of excellence above the clouds.

THREE YEARS LATER

Lizzie stood at the edge of the simulator, looking at the digital screen that was showing the open space outside of the plane.

Their instructor, Maureen, stood beside them, a supportive hand on Lizzie's shoulder.

"OK, I will count to three, the screen will flash red. When it flashes red, take a deep breath, hold it and then leap. The simulator will have the same air speed pushing towards you, so you will stay in the jump pit. Got it?"

Lizzie nodded.

"You've done this before, Lizzie. You can do it!"

Lizzie nodded again.

"One... two... three..."

Lizzie took a deep breath, held it, and then proceeded to jump straight outwards, feeling the immense air jet grab them and whip them into the air. Lizzie struggled to get into position, the power of the propulsive air tilting them up and down.

"Like we practiced, Lizzie!" Maureen yelled. The helmet and earmuffs protecting their head muffled the instructor's voice. Lizzie clenched, feeling their core muscles flex and stabilize their body position. Lizzie breathed calmly, looking below at the simulated atmosphere they were free falling through.

"OK. Here is the key part. Watch the spheres as they come toward you. If they are glowing light purple, leave them alone. Your future, your orb, will slowly flash the glowing color that means the most to your heart."

"What does that mean?" Lizzie yelled out, as simulated orbs began to float by.

Purple after purple after purple.

Queasiness started to settle in the pit of Lizzie's stomach.

Staring at each of the reflective orbs that went by, Lizzie wondered whose life was in each, and what each one had within. A silicon device that contained the entirety of someone's existence floating into the ether and... gone.

Were they the lives of the generation of students snuffed out? The remnants of families and pets and children not brought into the world? Houses and jobs, vehicles and android servants that disappeared without a second thought after Empyrean's team cleansed the selection year?

Lizzie tried to shake the thoughts that pushed through their brain while attempting to focus on an orb that wasn't purple.

Too late.

A reddish hued circle slipped through Lizzie's peripheral vision and the simulator flashed bright orange while an alarm sounded, and the air dissipated until Lizzie was standing on the digital screen that had projected the atmosphere.

"NOOOOO!" Lizzie yelled, stamping both feet.

"It's alright," Maureen said, coming over to give them a hug.

"It's not alright. What if that happens in real life? This is just a simulation. What if I miss and don't grab my orb?"

The instructor stared at Lizzie, running some replies through her mind, trying to figure out the best way to shield the truth from the student.

"To be honest," Maureen said, "we don't know."

"Great," Lizzie replied, beginning to struggle with the clasps that did up the helmet.

"Leave it on, let's go again."

"No thanks."

"Seriously. Relaunch simulator," she called to the control room before Lizzie could complain some more.

A whirl sounded, followed by a countdown from twenty. Lizzie stepped back onto the platform.

Clicking the helmet clasp shut, Lizzie cleared their mind, focused on breathing, and tried to let the negativity out through their nostrils.

When the simulator sounded and the air was forced from the vents, Lizzie leaped ahead, feeling the weightless free fall begin.

Immediately memories flooded through their brain. Lizzie blinked, trying to focus as orb upon orb sailed by.

*

"You'll always be special," a mom says to their kid. The mom remains the same size, the kid growing and growing. Rain falls, years fly by, smiles fade to sad acceptances. The mom becomes frail. Fragile.

"Yes, but what am I?" the kid asks the mom, knowing any answer will never alleviate the pain that glows within their heart, the lightning that stabs into the soul.

"Special. You're special," the mom says, a tear falling as a cheek is caressed.

*

Lizzie snapped back, hearing the instructor yelling directions.

"Look for your color!"

Maureen yelled it over and over, to the point of exhausting Lizzie's desire to even participate.

Finally, spent, Lizzie let their arms fall and was hurled high in the chamber. The instructor slammed the emergency shut-off switch. Lizzie floated back to the floor.

"What was that?"

"I'm done."

"You can't be done, Lizzie."

"Do you think if I miss my orb, it'll be painless?"

Lizzie tossed the helmet to the instructor, walking away without a response.

2.

"I heard what happened."

Lizzie remained on the bench, knees pulled up against their chest. The sobs had stopped long ago.

"I shouldn't exist."

"Why?"

Lizzie's jump partner Eric stepped closer, feeling the buzz of excitement he always felt while in their presence. Lizzie had his heart and the connection he longed for may not be reciprocated. That fear of rejection was enough to keep him at a distance.

Lizzie didn't move, face turned towards the far wall.

Stepping beside Lizzie, he gave a playful nudge with his knee, hoping that it would be enough to get Lizzie to at least turn, see his face.

"I can't describe it. There's this weight pressing down. I know I'm going to jump, and I know my orb will sail past me, and then what? Another person turned to spectral dust."

Eric sat in front of Lizzie's shins. He put a gentle, comforting hand on a knee, hoping he wasn't overstepping boundaries.

"Lizzie, we only have this one life to live. We're getting older. Soon, we might very well be jettisoned or incinerated if they didn't believe we had a role to fulfill here at home. You have to feel this? Our life passing us by? We need to jump, to see the color and grab it. Only then will we realize what we were supposed to do all along. Don't you want to see what your life should've been? What it can be?"

A hitched sob sounded in the dark. Lizzie wiped their wet cheeks. They placed a hand on top of Eric's. A squeeze, a joined acceleration of breathing. A shared closeness that felt forbidden.

Lizzie shifted, head now leaning against his shoulder.

"My mom always told me I was special."

"You are. She was an amazing woman. Without her insight into a number of areas, who knows where we might be now as a species."

"I just wish she was still here."

Eric nodded. They all did.

"Eric?"

"Yeah, Lizzie?"

"Do you ever feel like each moment we live erases a moment from our past?"

He let out a sigh.

"Yes."

"Is our time here speeding up? We're closer to our jump date than when we began our time in the program. I'm afraid for what's to come."

"I'm not. I can't wait. We've only ever been told about this in class. But to *actually* be one of the chosen? Phenomenal. We're lucky to be selected."

"Are we? I'm broken. None of this is forever. I'm not whole, not complete."

Eric leaned over, kissed Lizzie's forehead. Standing, he walked over to the exit.

"I'm always here for you Lizzie. You know that. I wish I'd have listened to every sound you've ever made, so that I could think about you for the rest of time. Remember how you smelled, your touch, your movements. We'll get through this together. Take a sleeping pill, recharge. Tomorrow, we'll do a tandem simulator jump. One step at a time. Together."

Lizzie nodded in the dark.

"That sounds like a plan," they said, Lizzie's voice flat and uninspired.

"Goodnight," Eric said, not knowing what else to say.

Lizzie walked into the simulator room, the spirits inside their head not leaving.

The stars shone brightly in the distance, a vision of a dying dream.

Eric sat in his jumpsuit, helmet on, holding Lizzie's.

He smiled. Lizzie returned an attempt.

"You ever feel lost? Like you can't be found?"

Eric sighed, wishing the new day had brought a different outlook.

"No, Lizzie. I can't say I have. You really are struggling, aren't you?"

Lizzie was crying again, waves washing over them. Each sob added an additional layer of anxiety and sorrow.

"I can't remember what she looks like, but I see her every night. I can't remember what my face looks like before... when I was just..."

Lizzie fell into Eric's arms, exhausted from the stress that had been building.

"Your darkness will go away, Lizzie. It will. The future is here, it's waiting for us. If you're lost, we'll find a way. We need to have hope. Hope tells us that it'll be OK. I swear."

Lizzie nodded against his chest.

"OK. OK, let's do this," Lizzie said, sounding confident and ready to tackle the task at hand.

"I know it gets harder every day, as we get closer to the actual jump. Other students are going through this as well. We can only control what's right before our eyes."

Lizzie nodded, putting the helmet on their head and clicking the clasps shut, locking it in place.

"You two ready?" Maureen said, giving them a firm pat on their shoulders.

They both gave a thumbs up, stepping to the edge of the simulator.

The countdown began. Each time the voice spoke a number it rolled through Lizzie like a drumbeat.

Ten...*boom*...nine...*boom*...eight...*boom*...

LCD screens flashed and flickered, various directions scrolling, popping out and fighting for leverage in the reader's eyes. Lizzie squinted, breath hitching and rolling like a train on the tracks. Panic festered and bloomed as the question began to dance behind eyes looking a thousand miles away.

What happens if I don't catch my orb?

"Ready?" Eric asked, taking Lizzie's hand and setting his feet into position. Lizzie looked over, got set and when the simulator launched, their entire vision took them to a place they'd long since forgotten.

4.

The grass is a deep green, so lush there is an unspoken law to only walk on it without shoes. You kick everything off on the sidewalk, socks and all, and feel the heavenly sensation of each blade caressing the soles of your feet as you dance.

A smile was always on Lizzie's face when they visited. How could it not be? Grandma's place was the pinnacle of childhood decadence. Candy in dishes to take as you wished, and toys in the corner where you played to your heart's content.

The adults left you alone – except Grandma. She'd come over and give Lizzie a hug or a kiss and ask how they were doing. Good, Lizzie would reply, their smile a smaller version of the elderly's.

A thought came into the little one's head then, a thought that continued to dominate them in the future.

"Grandma, what happens if you don't catch your orb?"

The lady makes a pssshhh sound, telling the child to not think of such things.

"Is mommy sick?"

"She is," Grandma replies, taking her time to sit on the floor beside Lizzie. "Her doctors are doing everything they can to make sure she gets better."

"No, she won't," Lizzie replies, causing a stern look to cross her Grandma's face.

"Now, Lizzie! Why would you say such a thing?"

"I see it when I close my eyes. And I see that I miss my orb."

Lizzie gets up and runs from the house, out onto the green grass. The Elder Level on the revolving ship is usually a calm space for habitants, but in one house, in one room, for one person, a sense of despair bathes over them while they sit on the floor.

5.

Lizzie found a return through the haze.

The air whooshed past, the orbs dancing in the LCD display.

"LIZZIE!" Eric yelled again. Lizzie was sure he'd been yelling for some time. His voice sounded hoarse, a result of repetitively screaming Lizzie's name over the cacophony they found themselves in.

Lizzie extended a hand. Their fingers intertwined and then steadied. Lizzie focused, looking at the oncoming orbs, and spotted a subtle light blue shift in one amongst the purple.

Letting go of Eric's hand, Lizzie pushed their arms out wide before closing them around the circular sphere.

SUCCESS-SUCCESS-SUCCESS

The voice boomed from speakers all around as the simulator powered down, and Lizzie could hear the jubilant shouts of excitement from the instructor and the control room.

This was Lizzie's 175th attempt in the simulator since being selected for Salvation. This was the first time they were successful in grabbing their orb.

Stepping out of the simulator, smiles greeted the two jumpers.

"You did it!" Maureen yelled, wrapping her arms tightly around Lizzie. Lizzie went along for the ride, but wasn't feeling the same sense of relief they saw on everyone else's faces.

Eric offered a high five and Lizzie returned it, the efforts of a smile forcing the edges of their lips up.

Eric could see it in Lizzie's eyes. The distant disinterest of the event.

"OK, before everyone comes and bruises Lizzie's shoulders with celebratory punches, I think we need to head to debrief. Lizzie's never been before, after all."

Nods all around were followed by spoken congratulations, as Lizzie unclipped the helmet, setting it beside Eric's.

The two left the simulator, one happier than the other.

As they made their way down the hall, up the elevator, and down more halls, they remained silent, the thrum of the revolving levels the only constant background noise.

Finally, Eric looked over, saw a returned glance and spoke.

"Oh, come off it, that was exciting, wasn't it?"

"I guess," Lizzie replied.

"You guess? You guess! You caught a fucking orb, Lizzie," the rarely used F-word getting the reaction Eric hoped for, Lizzie laughing and letting go of the armor that had shielded their face.

"I did. And it should've made me feel *something*, shouldn't it?"

They met eyes and remained that way until the elevator door dinged open.

Stepping through, they were silent, the piano strains of the elevator music filling the space above them.

Two hundred levels sailed by as they stood motionless, feeling the slow-down for their level after a few minutes.

Finally, it stopped, the doors opened, and they stepped out, standing before the glass entrance to the Debriefing Level.

"After you," Eric said, pulling one of the doors open and letting Lizzie enter.

*

The Debriefing Level was the most unsettling level, other than the Incinerator-Jettison Level, on the ship. It was cold, metallic and the buzz of the VR Headsets left a copper taste in the back of one's mouth.

A screen greeted them, asking for official identification. Eric scanned his card first, watching as his photo appeared, followed by his vital statistics and simulation results.

Name: Eric. Height: 6-0. Weight: 175lbs. Sex: Male. Success: 125. Failure: 12.

Lizzie stepped up next, cringing when the machine beeped as it read the card.

Name: Lizzie. Height: 5-4. Weight: 129lbs. Sex: NB. Success: 1. Failure: 174.

Access granted, a soft voice said, the door to the right of the monitor opening.

The two stepped through the opening into a hallway. Fluorescent lights illuminated the space beyond necessity, and the grates that made up the floor *clanked* and *thunked* with each boot strike.

When they reached the first door on the right of the hallway, a screen illuminated, and Eric's face appeared.

"This one's for me," he said, stepping through. Lizzie remained there until the door had closed and they were alone.

Lizzie walked to the next door, watching as their picture appeared and the door opened.

Unsure what to expect, Lizzie gazed into the darkened room as though it was the blackness of space.

"Welcome, Lizzie," a calming robotic voice said, as low light raised along the walls. In the center of the room sat a sterile looking chair, medical in nature and design. Before it, at head level, was a large device, which Lizzie knew to be the VR set that would sit atop the patient's head during the debrief. The buzzing grew louder the longer Lizzie stood there, the internal shouting of the brain telling them to run growing with each nanosecond.

"Please, do sit. We can begin."

Lizzie approached the chair with unease, expecting chains to burst forward and wrap around wrists and ankles, holding them down until despair finally brought reprieve.

When nothing happened, Lizzie saddled the seat and found the piece of furniture far more comfortable than first impressions suggested.

"Please place the VR set over your head. The set will auto adjust for size and weight so that it will feel virtually weightless. Once you hear the chime, close your eyes while the ocular approximator sets the light brightness for your debriefing session. A second chime will sound, at which time you may open your eyes and meet your clinician."

Lizzie reached out and grabbed the headset, feeling the resistance of the mechanical workings as it was placed over their head. Lowering both hands to rest comfortably on their lap, the headset calibrated and positioned itself with pinpoint accuracy. Lizzie thought it was not far off from a technician using the older generation of X-Ray devices. A chime sounded, eyes closed and beyond the eyelids lights flashed and flickered, the ocular approximator doing its job to ensure the session would be to the patient's comfort level.

A second chime sounded, Lizzie's eyes opened and before them were a man and woman, both dressed in a white dress shirt and black dress pants.

"Hello, Lizzie," they said in unison.

"Hello," came the reply.

"Welcome, to your very first debriefing session. This is a very exciting time for you, now that you've had a successful orb connection. My name is Dr. Natasha Light, and this is Dr. Randall Glow. We are here to help you understand absorption and work towards your future. Would you like to begin?"

Lizzie stared at the woman, wondering why such a sense of calm came over them while Dr. Light spoke.

"I guess so. I just don't know what I'm supposed to do."

"That's fair," Dr. Glow said, stepping a bit closer to Lizzie. "We'll walk you through initial setup, and then we can go from there. First things first. Who would you like to speak with? Myself or Dr. Light?"

Lizzie looked from one to the other, not realizing a decision was required.

"I really don't know. Do I have to make a choice?"

"Yes."

"OK, then I choose Dr. Light."

"Best of luck with your future, Lizzie," Dr. Glow said, before he nodded at Dr. Light and walked off screen. The sound of a door closing signified his exit, and Lizzie looked back to the smiling woman.

"Shall we begin?"

"How?"

"Well, let's go back to the start."

6. Back

"What is your earliest memory?"

Lizzie let their brain bring forth sights and sounds, smells and emotions.

Then, something settled into the forefront of them all.

"My earliest memory is me standing in a room but not. It's as though I'm a ghost."

"A ghost?"

*

A cold, uninviting room is all around young Lizzie, the walls bare and stark-white. A single window is on the wall to the left. Two steps and Lizzie is looking through the glass. The landscape is barren; light brown sand as far as the view spans. The sensation of centrifugal force makes Lizzie re-examine the floor. A stumble-step and outreached arms keep them upright, but the walls spin and then they are standing in the center of the room while an adult barks an order.

Collapsing, Lizzie tries to see the face, but the eyes look through the child, a ghost before an unbeliever.

"I'm right here," Lizzie speaks, wanting the adult to acknowledge them, but more shouted words and angry mannerisms suggest that Lizzie has become translucent and imperceptible.

The window slides open, squeals, while unseen creatures caress the wind that drops the temperature in the already cold room and the adult stomps over and slams it shut. When they turn, they finally register Lizzie standing there.
"Where were you?"
"Right here."
"Don't lie."
Before Lizzie can reply, the adult leaves the room, closing and locking the door behind them.

*

"Do you know who that adult was?" Dr. Light asked. When Lizzie looked, they found that Dr. Light was now sitting on a chair, left leg crossed over her right, notepad on her lap.

It was an odd thing to see. Lizzie didn't remember paper, or the use of paper for anything anymore, but somehow, they knew exactly what it was.

"Why do I know that the thing on your lap is a notepad?"

Dr. Light smiled, looked at the pad, flipped some pages before looking back at Lizzie.

"We try to create a calm environment and a safe place for debriefings, especially the first one. The VR set allows the use of low light ocular suggestions to the subconscious so that things are familiar."

"You can brainwash me?"

"Ha! No, no. Nothing like that."

Dr. Light's sudden laugh surprised Lizzie, but also acted to reassure that they were a real person and not a simulation.

"Dr. Light, where are you? Why don't we do this face-to-face?"

"Excellent question. I am located on the Medical Level. We are stationed here for our own safety.

People react to debriefings in a few ways. It might be a euphoric experience for some, or it may greatly disturb them. Because of the unknown way they may react, we stay separated at first to prevent any potential violent outbursts or injuries. It may sound arrogant, but the doctors and therapists living here are prized citizens for their knowledge and training. We need to be protected."

"Makes sense," Lizzie replied.

"You don't sound confident."

"Should I?"

"I'm here to help you, Lizzie. Nothing more."

"Why do you and Dr. Glow have last names but I don't have one?"

"It's a category thing. If you became a Doctor or a Dentist, you'd be gifted a last name as well."

"That's strange."

"Is it?"

"I don't trust a lot of people."

"Do you trust Eric?"

Lizzie wasn't sure why, but the prospect of Eric being mentioned hadn't occurred. It created a dagger-into-the-heart effect, forcing them to sit up straighter on the rigid chair.

"I do. Absolutely."

"Do you love Eric?"

Lizzie felt both cheeks flush, having never considered the question.

"Maybe... but more like an older brother?"

"You don't sound confident."

"I'm not."

"You never had siblings, did you?"

*

The white room returns before Lizzie's eyes. Now a bed is in one corner, another across from it. A girl plays with a doll while Lizzie watches their movements, unsure how to interact.

"Stop watching me," the girl says, face pulled back as though having spotted something repulsive.

"Can I play?" Lizzie asks, swinging both legs over the side of the bed.

"No," comes the reply, the girl now singing a song to her doll, her voice so low Lizzie can't hear the words.

Lizzie watches as time speeds up. New girls call the bed across from them home for a very short time, as they come and go with such rapidity that names and faces blur into a container of spilled paint. All the while Lizzie remains, sitting, watching, waiting.

*

"No. I never knew my parents."

"How did it feel to end up as a Ward of the government?"

"I never knew what that meant. I never knew what a mom or dad was."

"Until your mom adopted you?"

Lizzie felt a panic growing. Tears were about to come.

"I'm going to cry. Is that OK?"

"It is, don't worry about the VR set. People cry while attached all the time."

"Thank you," Lizzie whispered, thinking back to the arrival of their mom.

*

Lizzie sits on the edge of the bed, alone in the room. The other bed had long been removed, all the other Wards who'd been abandoned on the revolving ship long since adopted out.

All but Lizzie.

The door opens, a man and woman step into the room.

"Lizzie, would you like to come outside with us? There's someone who would like to meet you."

Lizzie nods, slides from the bed, fails to put on shoes.

They lead the child from the room, down a short hallway to an access door. A card is swiped, a hand scanned, and a four-digit code typed in. The door hisses and pops open. The adults push it further open, waiting until it has swung fully to the side, before the three make their way down some steps and stand in the sand. Lizzie is perplexed. The bottoms of their feet have only experienced tile. Sand is a new sensation, and without any shoes on, ten toes wiggle and take it in. Before the adults can say anything to stop them, Lizzie runs and jumps in the wide-open space, sending sand flying all around.

Someone joins Lizzie. They are running, jumping, laughing and throwing sand along with the child. Lizzie looks, seeing a beautiful woman. Long black hair, dark eyes, a smile that warms their heart. Lizzie leaps into the woman's arms, the hug a moment of predestined euphoria that sends a message from child to adult and back again.

We are whole, *it says.* We are meant to be one. Together.

The woman kneels, letting go of the child. She smiles, Lizzie reciprocates. It's only then that Lizzie spots the insignia of the Higher Levels on the woman's shirt.

The two adults have now arrived, both giving Lizzie a lecture on respecting royalty and acting appropriately.

"Enough," the woman says, shutting them both up instantly.

"Lizzie, would you like to come live with me?"

"Very much. Yes, please."

She stands, taking Lizzie's hand.

The two walk away from the adults, Lizzie aware of a man walking with them, but not paying close attention.

Lizzie leaves the Ward Level behind, never to return.

*

"You miss your mom, don't you?" Dr. Light asked, shaking Lizzie clear of the memory.

"Of course."

"Do you think you'll find your mom in your orb?"

The question shattered Lizzie's understanding of what the orb contains.

"Excuse me? That's a possibility?"

"Maybe. You see, the orb is for you to grasp and absorb. We don't know where or when it'll transport you to your 'future'," she said, emphasizing future with air quotes. "You may relive your life or purely go from the point of absorption and live from that day on. It really is quite fascinating."

"What if you don't catch one? What if I miss?"

"Do you think that'll happen?"

"I've missed 174 times, haven't I? Why will no one answer what happens if I miss?"

"Why do you think people won't answer?"

"Either you don't know, or for some reason you won't tell me."

"Honestly, I don't know. I can ask some colleagues and see if they know. Does that work?"

"I guess."

"Tell me about your mom."

"What do you want to know?"

"Did she think you were a ghost?"

"No. She thought I was special."

*

A river flows through the heart of the High Level. Royalty comes and goes, sitting at the edge, some wading into it. Lizzie has never seen water like this before. Each day is a new achievement of sensations and experiences.

Lizzie sits on a bench, while nearby a lady plays an instrument.

"Mom, what are those?"

She looks at where Lizzie is pointing, smiling when she sees the birds.

"Birds, my dear Lizzie. They are animals. Oh, the wonders that Earth used to provide."

"What are they doing?"

"They are flying in the sky. A bird uses its two wings to propel itself. Much like how we run, they fly. Truly amazing, isn't it?"

Lizzie nods excitedly, watching the creatures swoop and dive.

"Shall we go have some lunch?"

The two return to their home, a strange thing for Lizzie to comprehend.

A home. Where Lizzie has a room all to themselves.

A mom. Lizzie has a mom.

Lost in the substance of those ideas, Lizzie is surprised when arms wrap around them and suddenly Lizzie is spinning and laughing.

"Mom, put me down!"

Collapsing in a pile of laughter and tears, the two hug and remain together, their hearts connected and beating in sync.

"Lizzie. You are so special. I'll never tell you otherwise. I've never loved anyone like the love I have for you."

Lizzie snuggles in closer, enveloped by the warmth only a mother can offer.

*

"How do you feel about being selected for Salvation?" Dr. Light asked.

"My first thought was 'why me?' My second thought was, 'what does it matter, I'm not going to catch my orb anyways?'"

"Do you think your defeatist ideology is because of being a Ward and constantly being passed over?"

"Yes."

*

Lizzie sits beside the river, watching kids play. They frolic and wrestle as only children of that age can. Lizzie keeps looking for a way in, a point to inject themselves into their activities to allow for inclusion.

"Just go ask," Mom says, giving Lizzie's shoulder a nudge with her own.

"No thanks."

"You'll never know unless you try."

"They can't reject me if they're not given the opportunity."

"Now, Lizzie. Bug. You need to try a little, yeah? You're infinitely special. Some friends other than me would do you some good."

"No thanks," Lizzie replies, standing and walking back towards their home.

"Then how about school? There are classes I can enroll you in?"

"If I enroll in school, I'll be in the pool for Salvation or Eradication, won't I?"

"You will."
"Do it."

*

"How did you find school?"
"Hated it."

7. School

School took up two levels of the revolving ship.

The first level was for the starters, the second for the finishers. It was a mishmash of ages, all co-mingling and learning ideas and teachings together.

On Lizzie's first day, they sat beside Savannah.

Savannah, even at just twelve years old, was stunningly attractive. Lizzie felt an odd attraction, as those at the beginning of sexual maturity would find. Something about Savannah excited them, but what exactly? Well, that was unknown.

"Hey."

Lizzie hadn't expected anyone to talk to them, let alone on the first day, so when Savannah spoke, it was a surprise.

"Sorry, did you just speak to me?"

"I did. My name's Savannah."

"Oh... uh... Lizzie. Everyone calls me Lizzie."

"Nice to meet you Lizzie."

An unexpected friendship was fostered from that tentative initial introduction.

Each day, Savannah waited for Lizzie's arrival at school. They sat beside each other in class, ate lunch together, and waited together after the last bell. Savannah never asked about Lizzie *leaving through the Royal's Only Elevator, nor about Lizzie's mom. Lizzie never asked Savannah about her background. They were just two friends who laughed about silly things and shared what they thought their futures held.*

Still, each night, Lizzie gets home and when Mom asks how the day went, Lizzie finds they hated it.

"I don't learn enough. Our teacher focuses so much on what it would mean if we are selected for Salvation. I don't care. I want to learn."

"Being taught about Salvation is learning, Lizzie. You need to open your mind and allow your teacher to share things unrestricted. Going in with a prejudice won't allow you to grow and adapt."

*

"Your mom was a smart lady," Dr. Light said. Lizzie saw she was smiling.

"She was."

"Savannah sounds like a great friend. Do you still see her?"

"I do. Not as much as I would like. She's on the Labor Level now."

"How did that happen?"

"Her mom grew scared that our class would be selected for Eradication. So, she arranged for a job for Savannah and removed her from school."

"How did that make you feel, when Savannah was removed?"

"Lost. Like my best friend had been ripped away. Jettisoned."

"Why do you think Empyrean chooses classes for Salvation or Eradication, Lizzie?"

The question was unexpected. No one had ever discussed this before, nor had the question been one they'd thought about in any great depth.

"I wouldn't know. Maybe this is something we need to ask Mr. Eldridge?"

Dr. Light nodded, appearing to write something on the pad before her.

"Have you been taking notes this whole time?"

"I have."

"Why?"

"Because you're fascinating. And because, as your debriefer, I will need to file my findings in your chart."

"Why do you find me fascinating?"

"I'm afraid I can't discuss that. Are you working to deflect away from my Empyrean question? Would you like to know why?"

"I would."

"When the world crumbled, the human race faced a decision. Empyrean had already successfully launched the off-world revolving ship, which we call home. But it wasn't as immense nor as spectacular as it is now. Mr. Eldridge had put provisions in place for a slow development, but when the grids began to fail, the oceans rose and society dissolved, that plan was accelerated. To the point that the revolving ship quadrupled in size in the first year and then quadrupled again the following year. The ship is sustainable, but only to a degree. Mr. Eldridge always believed we'd return to Earth."

"If you grab your orb, do you return to Earth?"

"Is that what you believe?"

"I don't know."

Dr. Light scribbled some more on her pad, before taking a drink from a glass that Lizzie hadn't noticed was beside her. *Had the table it sat on been there this whole time?*

"Lizzie, did you know we have an Expedition Level?"

"No. What's that?"

"In the Before Time, the old world, they had people called Astronauts. Astronauts were specialists trained to leave Earth and go into outer space. Empyrean has an Expedition Level where specialists, known as Returners, make trips to the surface to analyze the environment. They are key in us returning to live on the surface."

"That's amazing."

"It truly is. Do you know what they've been finding?"

"No, how would I? I didn't know they were a thing until you just told me."

"That's fair. The Returners have been finding the planet has reclaimed itself. The buildings humans built all those years ago have been overrun, no longer visible. The concrete jungles that you see in old news stories and teachings simply don't exist anymore. It is as though humans never built a single thing, never existed on the planet."

"If we've been sending classes all of these years to jump and catch their orbs, where are they?"

"Where do you think they are?"

"Oh, for fuck's sake. Seriously, Dr. Light? Please just answer the question instead of asking another?"

Dr. Light put up her hands in submission, the look on her face remaining calm.

"I'm sorry, Lizzie. You've been selected to jump. We need to push your buttons and see your responses. Some of my replies are meant to engage and some are meant to enrage. Empyrean can only sustain a specific number of people on the revolving ship for so many years."

"Is that why people who commit crimes are jettisoned?"

"Correct."

"So, if we're being honest with each other, Dr. Light, it doesn't matter if a class is selected for Salvation or Eradication. We're all jettisoned from the ship."

"Correct."

Lizzie started to remove the VR set, an aqua alarm flashing on the screen.

"Please stop, Lizzie. This session is far from over."

"I don't care, Dr. Light. I'm a nobody. Inconsequential. I was 'selected' but really, it's just another way for the powers that be to get rid of people, so they don't have to feed them."

"Lizzie, it's not like that. Empyrean wants you to live a full and amazing life. That's why the orbs are there. You're selected to catch one, to live an amazing life and enjoy whatever it is you discover in absorption."

"But what if I miss my orb?"

Dr. Light looked to be contemplating a response, when Dr. Glow re-entered the screen before Lizzie. He gave a quick wave, before whispering into Dr. Light's ear. To Lizzie's surprise, he gave Dr. Light a kiss on the cheek before departing.

"Are you two... together?"

"We are."

"Has he been listening the entire time?"

"No. Dr. Glow has been in another session. He came in to pass on some information that I've been instructed to share with you. Mr. Eldridge was very close with your mom. Great respect for her. He's asked that we share what we know with you about the orb and absorption."

"Mr. Eldridge is still alive? How old is he?"

"Unknown. Truthfully, I don't know if he is alive physically or purely consciously. No one has seen him in person for many, many years."

"I met him once."

*

Lizzie is standing in the kitchen. Mom is making bacon, which is a rare delicacy, as only Royals have access to pork products once a decade.

Someone clears their throat behind Lizzie. Turning, they find a man who is instantly recognizable.

"Mr. Eldridge. An honor," Lizzie says, bowing to the High Royal and Creator of the ship.

"Lizzie, no need for such formalities, but it's great to see your mother has taught you so well."

He steps forward, extending a hand. For a second, Lizzie is startled, before realizing he simply wants to shake hands. When they do so, Lizzie finds his hand cold and stiff, as though his body is beginning to rot.

"What gives us the privilege of your presence this morning?"

"Your mother is trying to help me with an... issue. Being the smartest person on the ship, only she can solve this riddle."

"I see. Morning, Mom."

"Morning, love."

Lizzie sits and eavesdrops on the adults, hearing some of their hushed back and forth.

It doesn't take long for Lizzie to understand what's happening.

"Will my mom get sick too?"

Both adults stop speaking. Neither turn to look at Lizzie, both trying to formulate their reply.

It was Lizzie's mom who answered.

"We believe so. Unless I can find a formula to stop how it affects us on a cellular level."

"How long do you have, Mr. Eldridge?"

"We don't know. Weeks? Days?"

"I hope you can help him, Mom."

Lizzie leaves them to talk.

Returning to their room, Lizzie crawls back under the sheets and closes both eyes, wishing they'd never entered the kitchen.

*

"He is an amazing man," Dr. Light said.

"I'm sure he was."

Dr. Light didn't take the bait thrown her way with the use of *was*. Instead she flipped through her notepad, took another drink and then looked back at Lizzie.

"Tell me more about Savannah."

8. Savannah

"I'm sorry my mom is taking me out of school."

Lizzie and Savannah are sitting together on an Observation Level, watching the Earth rotate before them. The edge of the sphere was always something Lizzie loved examining. Seeing the light illuminate the clouds and the land below filled them with a surreal scope of enormity. As though something this massive shouldn't exist so close to them, out in the vast open space.

Turning, Lizzie finds Savannah's teary eyes. Leaning in, they share a tentative kiss, a secret kept from all others. Lizzie wipes the water from Savannah's cheeks before moving closer. Feeling Savannah's body heat was always reassuring. The thought that it wouldn't be happening much longer was driving a spear between Lizzie's lungs.

"She's just trying to protect you. Decision day is coming soon. Salvation or Eradication. Either way... our lives as we know it will end."

"But I don't want to live without you."

"I do love you."

"I know."

"I'm sorry I'm staying in school."

"I know."

"Look at how stunning the water on Earth looks today," Lizzie says.

"You've never been a ghost to me, Lizzie," Savannah replies. "I knew how special you were the very first day we met."

"I know."

They sit and watch the Earth spin for the next few hours, until the ship's timed power reduction dims the lights, and a soft voice suggests all inhabitants return to their Sleeping Levels.

"Would you like to come spend the night at my home?" Lizzie asks, knowing the answer as soon as the question was asked.

"Maybe some other time. My mom is expecting me. I'll see you soon," said Savannah, the two sharing one last kiss.

Lizzie watches her walk away, towards the elevator heading lower.

Another lonely night would be spent in the silent house. Lizzie had decided to remain there after Mom passed away, even if it meant an existence eerily similar to living on the Ward Level.

*

"When was the last time you spoke with Savannah?" Dr. Light asked.

"I haven't."

"Since she told you she was leaving school?"

"Yeah."

"Why haven't you?"

"Not sure. I feel like maybe it's better that we parted on such sweet terms than for her to know I've been chosen for Salvation and that we only have so much time together before I jump."

"Do you think you're ready for Salvation?"

"Salvation or Eradication, either way I'd be leaving the ship. What's left here for me? Mom's gone."

"Savannah is still here. So is Eric."

"I can't love others if I'll never love myself."

"Why do you believe that?"

"Look at me. I'm just *me*. Mom may have said I'm special, but being special didn't save her. Being special isn't going to keep me here with Savannah or Eric. I'm going to be jumping. When I miss my orb, then what?"

"Lizzie, you have two people who care deeply about you. If I could put in a request to have your Salvation revoked and have you live your life on the Labor Level, would you want that?"

"You can do that?"

"I can."

"Would you?"

"If you asked."

"If I stayed, would someone else be selected?"

"No."

"Then I'll jump."

"Why?"

"If I stayed and someone else wouldn't be selected, that would mean by default, someone else would be jettisoned, correct?"

Dr. Light's lips pursed; her shoulders shifted. Her eyes darted back and forth.

"Correct."

"I'd rather sacrifice myself than someone else. That would be awfully selfish of me to stay and willingly kill someone else."

"That is a very responsible way to approach it."

"More responsible than Empyrean's approach."

Dr. Light remained silent; her gaze was telling Lizzie that she was on the edge of an outburst herself.

"Let's get back on track. Tell me about Eric."

"Why?"

"I want to know more."

"I thought you were going to tell me about the orbs and absorption?"

"I will. First, tell me about Eric. He's going to be your jump partner. He's been very efficient in his simulation tests. When did you first meet?"

"In class. He sat on the far side of the room. We never spoke until Savannah left."

"Why was that?"

"He said I intimidated him."

*

The first day that Lizzie arrived at class without Savannah was strange.

She wasn't waiting for Lizzie. She wasn't sitting beside Lizzie's desk. They didn't eat lunch or whisper to each other while the day went on.

It wasn't until Lizzie was leaving at the end of the day that someone spoke to them.

"It's Lizzie, right?"

Lizzie turned and saw one of the older students standing there, smiling.

"Uh... yeah. Eric, right?"

"Wow didn't think you knew my name. Where's your friend?"

"She's been pulled. She's on the Labor Level now."

"Oh, wow. I'm so sorry. I didn't know."

"That's OK."

"You mind if I walk with you to the elevators?"

"Why?"

Eric laughed, embarrassed and uncomfortable.

"I don't have many friends, and I've been meaning to introduce myself to you two."

"I see. Scared?"

"Yes."

Lizzie was surprised by his admission.

"Decision is coming soon."

"Yeah," he said and sighed. "I don't know how it'll go, but I don't want to die."

Lizzie nodded.

"Sometimes we can only accept that what's inside is a filled-up void."

"My heart feels colder. My parents don't seem to care either way. For them, one less mouth to feed, one less person under foot."

"My mom's dead."

Eric looked at Lizzie, having never met someone quite like them.

"You intrigue me, Lizzie."

"Sure."

"Sure?"

"Sure, let's walk."

The two walked towards the elevators, Lizzie wondering how Eric would respond when he got onto his elevator and Lizzie took the Royal one.

He was a good half-foot taller than Lizzie, but height didn't mean anything when you were eradicated.

"Which level do you live on?" he asked, pushing the button for his level.

"I have to take that elevator," Lizzie replied, pointing to the further one.

"Oh? Wow. I didn't realize."

"All good, no need to make a big deal out of it. I was a Ward who was adopted by a Royal."

"Ah. Well, I'll see you tomorrow?"

"You will."

The rest of the night, Lizzie was perplexed. Was it purely the attention shown from Eric that created excitement? Or was there an honest-to-goodness physical reaction?

The house had always felt hollow and forgotten when Lizzie returned home, but tonight it felt completely void of living energy. The abrupt leaving of Savannah and the introduction of Eric had created an internal chaos Lizzie would need to take some time to contemplate. Lizzie just wished the house was more inviting.

*

"Does it make you feel happy or sad that you're jumping with Eric?"

"Neither."

"How do you think it makes Eric feel?"

"Happy."

"How does it make you feel that Eric is happy about this?"

"Nothing. I feel nothing. I just want to jump, get it over with and find out what happens whether I catch my orb or I don't."

"Ahhh, so now you think you may catch it?"

"Seriously?"

"Lizzie, I need to try and mentally prepare you for that monumental moment."

"Have you ever been a Ward, Dr. Light?"

"No."

"Nothing can even come close to the sensation of someone accepting you and adopting you. Mom gave me that moment already. Now, I'm supposed to believe that leaping off the ship and catching my orb will be the greatest moment of my life? Doubt it."

"What if the future in the orb is with your mom?"

"You already suggested that, Dr. Light."

"And what did you answer?"

"What does it matter?"

"Do you think when Eric pictures his future in his orb that you're there beside him?"

"I've never considered that."

"Tell me more about Eric."

*

Lizzie knew that Eric had more than 'let's be friends' feelings from the start. He didn't make unwanted advances or anything like that, but Lizzie understood his intentions. Not that Lizzie was going to reciprocate those emotions, especially with longing for Savannah.

When Lizzie thought back on any definitive moments in their relationship, one stuck out more than anything. The day after the class had been selected, Eric had looked everywhere for Lizzie.

Lizzie had taken the elevator down to the Labor Level, but when the doors opened, the confidence to walk out and find Savannah had left immediately.

Lizzie returned to the dark house, most of the windows closed, the light restricted from illuminating the rooms beyond.

Sitting on a couch in the living space, Lizzie felt hopelessly lost. The desire to head to the Incinerator Level and burn up before being jettisoned appeared to be the best option.

A soft knock on the door surprised Lizzie, causing a hurried rush to the door and wide eyes once it was opened.

"Eric?"

"Hey."

"What're you doing up here?"

"I wanted to make sure you were alright."

"Thank you."

"Are you?"

"Nope."

He didn't ask for permission, just acted as a best friend should. Eric wrapped Lizzie into a hug, his huge frame engulfing the smaller one.

They sat and talked for some time. Lizzie shared more with Eric than even Savannah. Something had switched that allowed for unquestioned, implicit trust in him. On the cusp of adulthood, it was sorrowful to stop and think that neither of them had much time left on the revolving ship.

"Are you excited to jump?" Eric asked.

"Not at all. You?"

"Absolutely."

Silence visited them for some time, the ethereal stillness of two souls longing.

Eventually Eric stood, suggesting he would head home.

"You can spend the night here if you'd like," Lizzie replied, immediately regretting any connotation of sexual suggestion. "You've never seen what the night sky looks like from the Royal Level, have you?"

"No. I've never been to the High Levels before. I really shouldn't stay. I wouldn't want anyone to think anything impure about our friendship."

"OK. Thank you for coming, it does mean a lot."

Lizzie took his hand and squeezed it, feeling guilt immediately. A longing for Savannah reared up, but the warmth Eric caused within suppressed that.

Eric let himself out, plunging Lizzie back into the fragile emptiness the house now hosted.

*

"Lizzie, would you like to pause todays debrief here and meet again tomorrow?"

Lizzie hadn't believed that was an option.

"I thought we were here until we finished?"

"Nope. Debriefing is a key part of jump preparation. I think I've pushed you far enough today."

"OK. Do I just come here whenever?"

"Yes, you're my only client. We take on one member of the selected group for Salvation each time. When you scan in, I'll be summoned."

"So, is this your way of not sharing about the orbs?"

Dr. Light chuckled, waving her hand.

"We'll see how tomorrow goes."

They said their goodbyes, the VR set detaching and resetting. Lizzie stumbled off the hard seat, legs unsure and asleep. The numbness and tingling was an awkward sensation.

Outside of the debrief room, Lizzie had expected to find Eric, but instead discovered an empty space, the only sound the buzzing of the VR sets.

9. Home

Lizzie found Eric sitting on the front step of the shadow house.

"Hey," he said, standing when Lizzie approached.

Before another word was spoken, Lizzie stepped into Eric and kissed him. He drew back at the unexpected act, but then reciprocated once he saw that Lizzie wasn't playing a joke.

"Wow, Lizzie," Eric said, once he'd regained his composure.

"Sorry," came the reply.

"Don't be sorry. That was... amazing. But, seriously, I wasn't expecting that."

"I know it's something you've wished for. We don't have many days left together or even on the ship. I didn't want to not let you experience what you truly wanted but couldn't ask for."

"Lizzie, you are the strangest person I've ever met," Eric said, laughing.

"Thank you. Would you like to come inside? I can make us some dinner."

"No, thank you. I was stopping by to see if you were OK. I have to visit the nurses tonight to do blood work one more time before jump day. When do you need to do blood work?"

"I'm not sure, Dr. Light hasn't mentioned it. I'm seeing her tomorrow again."

"Ah, that explains it. You'll need to do it tomorrow after debriefing then. You ready for the big day?"

"No. You?"

"Absolutely."

Eric left, leaving Lizzie sitting on the steps of the house that no longer felt like a home, on a level of a ship that was expelling them in a few days. The Earth shared some of its beauty with Lizzie while sitting there, before getting up and entering.

An aching for Eric returned once in bed, but Lizzie shut both eyes and fell asleep.

10.

Lizzie felt strange returning to the Debriefing Level alone.

Checking in was straightforward, and shortly Lizzie was sitting in the chair looking at the smiling face of Dr. Light.

"Only one more day. Nervous?"

"Nope."

"Excited?"

"Nope."

"Anything?"

"Annoyed," Lizzie replied, which garnered a chuckle from the doctor.

"Did you have time to examine your thoughts on how you really feel about Eric?"

"I did. I told him and showed him last night that I love him."

Dr. Light's eyebrows raised, hearing Lizzie's description.

"Showed him? Dare I ask?"

"We kissed," Lizzie replied.

"I have to say, you've surprised me Lizzie. I didn't think you'd allow Eric the knowledge of your feelings. That's a very mature step."

"Can I go now?"

"No, no. I have a few more questions to ask you."

"Like what?"

"Well, tell me, when you jumped in the simulator and you successfully caught the orb, what did you sense in the simulated absorption?"

"Nothing."

"Nothing?"

"As soon as I caught it, the simulator sounded and everyone around me began screaming and cheering. Was I supposed to feel something?"

Dr. Light stared at Lizzie, face emotionless for an uncomfortably long time before speaking.

"Are you ever going to tell me the truth of the orbs? Absorption?"

"Do you really want to know what we think happens?"

"Wait? You don't actually know? Were you just leading me on then?"

"We know a little, Lizzie. No one's ever come back. What we do believe is..."

Lizzie made a pained noise. Frustration boiling over.

"Oh, hell. OK, I'm done for today. Am I to come back tomorrow? I'm assuming I need to simulate again and Eric mentioned blood work?"

"I'll see you tomorrow. No blood work yet."

11.

The elevator return trip to the Home Level was accompanied by an ominous feeling that had been sitting like a dense rock in Lizzie's stomach.

Something was off.

When the doors slid open, the level beyond was in full deterioration mode.

Lizzie knew that Empyrean would remodel the space once no one lived in it, but Lizzie was shocked to see that it had already begun. Maybe they'd believed Lizzie would've relocated by now in preparation for the big jump?

Sand whipped and blew as the nano-bots scuttled and scurried around, beginning to digest anything that was not stock level. The house was now a black shadow, the door unable to be seen from where Lizzie stood.

Would entrance even be permissible?

Approaching the house, Lizzie saw a shadowed figure move forth, their appearance startling and unbelievable.

"Mr. Eldridge?"

"Lizzie. Please, let's have a word."

12. Mr. Eldridge

Once Lizzie and Mr. Eldridge had entered the home, they remained silent as though both waiting for the other to speak first.

Lizzie couldn't look at the withered old man for long. Seeing him strapped into the motorized wheelchair was enough of a shock, but the translucent appearance of his purple-veined skin pushed it over the edge.

Lizzie couldn't even begin to imagine how old the man must be.

"How've you been, Mr. Eldridge?"

"Please, call me Albert."

"OK. How're you still alive, Albert?"

He smiled, yellowed teeth and grey gums exposed behind the thinnest of lips.

"Our existence is filled with wondrous things, Lizzie. Things you, nor I, truthfully, can even comprehend. I know your mother always said you were special, we just never knew how special."

"What does that even mean?"

"Your blood was the elixir I needed to remain alive. I am dying, slowly, but at such a glacial rate, I will most likely outlive all the people on my ship."

Lizzie slumped back against the counter, the hard edge digging into the soft area of the lower back, forcing a grimace. Eldridge took that as a sign to keep speaking, Lizzie deciding not to interrupt.

"The reason I've left my solitude on my Hidden Level was to come and say goodbye. Your Selection was never random. You gave me a gift that I could never repay. In return, I made sure you were selected."

"Wouldn't a nicer gift be, I don't know, not tossing me from your ship? Not destroying my mom's house, my home, even as I still live here?"

"The sands of time are cruel and consistent, Lizzie. This ship is failing. Earth is failing. What we have here is a living and breathing hourglass. The contents have been flowing from the top to the bottom for many years. Time is running out. I've been working round the clock for decades to try and figure out a fix, a way for our residents to remain living here, and living safely. But, the orbs. The orbs keep coming. The orbs are always an option for those I cherish most. Selection has never been random, each group has had a personal connection to me. Now, it is your turn. I wish you could live here now and forever, Lizzie, but that isn't an option."

"But why me? Why do I need to jump?"

"I can't risk someone else discovering the truth of your blood. Using it to outlive me or usurp me. You are a threat to me, Lizzie. Even if you never knew it."

"What happens if I miss my orb?"

Mr. Eldridge smiled and pushed the joystick controller on his wheelchair, whirling around to face the door.

The sound of the engine echoed in the space as though a panel of the ship had blown off.

"Albert? Please?"

"I would love to know, Lizzie. If that happens, make sure to tell me," he called over his shoulder as he exited the house. Beyond him, the landscape was unrecognizable, the nano-bots continuing their work.

Eric

*

"Do you remember when the bombs fell?"

"I do."

"Would you have changed anything? Done anything differently if you'd have known what was to come?"

"I wouldn't."

"No?"

"Sometimes chaos is necessary for rebirth."

*

13.

Lizzie knew Eric was standing outside of the house.
How?

The dream. Lizzie had the dream again of Eric speaking of destruction in his debriefing. *But was it a dream?* Or a memory somehow shared across synapses?

Lizzie stretched in bed, feeling the emptiness, longing for sensations foreign and delicious.

Declining to get dressed, Lizzie opened the door, finding Eric right where the dream had said he'd be.

"I've become rusted and decayed," Lizzie said. Eric looked over the nakedness presented before him.

"Lizzie, come on, let's get you dressed," he said, stepping inside. Closing the door to the carnage of the bots beyond, he found Lizzie's jump suit and helped get the limbs and torso within and covered.

"Dr. Light has sent me to retrieve you. Blood work is needed before tomorrow's jump."

"Of course, Eldridge will want more blood," Lizzie said angrily.

"They collect blood from us all. Not just you. Protocols must be followed."

"Why? What good are protocols anymore? Tomorrow we're done and gone. Forgotten and erased."

"Maybe from here, Lizzie, but not from ourselves."

Eric was practically pleading now, wanting to get the last few steps finished and completed so that he could prepare for his jump.

Lizzie wished beyond anything that they weren't jump partners. Eric looked into their eyes, deep into Lizzie's heart with his gaze, and it caused anger, not love.

"Fine. Let's go. For you. I wish I was never selected."

Even though it was said harshly, Eric smiled, happy that they were progressing in the right direction.

"Lizzie, it'll be truly amazing. I'm telling you. Our futures will be known tomorrow. We'll leap, we'll fall and then absorption and after... the rest of our lives will be there, laid out before us."

Lizzie had to admit his enthusiasm was contagious, but nothing was going to make this event exciting or something Lizzie longed for.

"Shall we watch?"

Eric took Lizzie's hand and they turned around, waiting at the entrance of the elevator. Before them, the house that had become Lizzie's home pixelated and flickered, the nano-bots devouring the last bit of coding that allowed for its existence. A desolate waste land of sand and memories was all that was left. Lizzie felt the burning prickle of a single tear spill out of an eye and down a cheek.

"Let's go," Eric said, stepping into the elevator.

Lizzie followed, preventing more anguish by not looking back.

14. Savannah

Stepping off the elevator at the Debriefing Level, Eric gave Lizzie a gentle push forward.

"Dr. Light is waiting."

Lizzie nodded, scanned in, and stood in the hallway.

Once the room signalled, Lizzie opened the door and repeated the already familiar VR set routine. Dr. Light's smiling face was soon on the screen.

"Hello, Lizzie. How're you today?"

"Absolute shit. My home is now gone."

"I'm aware. Necessary function for the ongoing usage of the ship. A new Royal has already begun to program what their new home will look like."

"New Royal?"

"Yes. Promotion occurs when an opening becomes available on the High Level. Your mother had a line of succession drawn up many years ago. In fact, she'd listed Savannah's mother as the next to become a Royal when the time came. This was years before you were adopted, of course."

"Does that mean Savannah will live on the High Level? Is she also a Royal?" Lizzie was surprised with the emotion carried on each spoken word.

"No. Her mother will be, yes, but Savannah, much like yourself will not be a Royal by label. She will have access to the ship, just like you did, and if her mother allows her to live on the High Level, then she will. Otherwise, Savannah will continue to work on the Labor Level."

"I see."

"How does that make you feel?"

"Undefined."

"Undefined?"

"If Savannah gets to live on the High Level, I'm very happy for her. If not, then I'm sad. Savannah means more to me than any other person I've ever met, except Mom. I want nothing but her happiness. But on the other side of things, I'm still jumping tomorrow."

"You are."

"Mr. Eldridge came to visit me."

Dr. Light's eyes flickered a brief second of shock before regaining composure. Lizzie thought for sure she would've known about the visit.

"He did?"

"Yes. Yesterday."

"How was that?"

"He's old."

Dr. Light laughed at this.

"We know that. But *how* is he?"

"Dying. He told me my blood is special and that it was the reason he's been able to remain living for all of these years."

"How long ago did your mom adopt you?"

"I'm not sure. I should know, but I can't remember. Maybe fifteen years?"

"Yes. Fifteen years is correct. You were five when she took you home from the Ward Level. I would agree with him, Lizzie. If your blood has prolonged his life by another fifteen years, that's truly remarkable. Very special."

"Is that why I'm supposed to do blood work today?"

"No, no. Every student who has been selected provides blood. It's a way for us to catalog the species and trace relatives."

"I don't know if I believe that."

"Shall we move on? I have two last questions I'd like to go over with you before you can get blood done and then head to your acceptance ceremony."

"Fine. What are they?"

"I must say, Lizzie, you're the first selected student I've ever had in debriefing who wasn't happy they were chosen."

"Does that mean I don't have to do another simulation today?"

"That's fair. I'll cancel the simulation, but you still need to do blood."

"So, what's the first question?"

"What is your most frequent dream?"

*

The boy and the girl had slept peacefully.

The room was circular in shape, as though it presented a beginning, a middle, and an end that was infinitely occurring.

The boy's bed was hard and lumpy.

The girl's soft and comfortable.

They never questioned it, nor spoke up about it. It was how it was. As it always had been.

A boy needs to be hard.

A girl soft.

The sun rose, waking them up, beckoning them to leave the room, leave the walls and make their way outside.

There, they stood, staring at the world before them.
Bright. Full of smells, sounds and color.
Vibrant.
The bombs that soared high above left a plume trail behind as they arced ever higher overhead.
The greens and blues and purples were soon to become reds and oranges and yellows.
Nature into flames.
The girl felt a sorrow filling up the space where other emotions usually rested.
The boy smiled, wanting to see the impending destruction.
Beyond the bombs, above the atmosphere, the moon shone down, as did the sun. Everywhere they looked it was filled with stars and hope.
"Does it look like what's in your head?"
"Every little bit."
"Could you imagine a picture more beautiful?"
"Not in my wildest dreams."
They skipped across the grass, relishing the moment.
The grass tickled their soles, the sun warmed their skin. Smiles were wide, teeth glimmered. As they ran and laughed, everything they'd ever seen, heard and smelled rushed into their brains, the blood threatening to burst in an embolism of sensory overload.
"Stop. Wait. Detonation is about to happen."
Sitting down, legs crossed, arms slack, the bombs reached the apex, man finally at the precipice of its existence.
"Did you think we wouldn't grow up?"
"I never thought we'd live life on such an easy street."
"We were given everything in a silver cup."

"At the end of the day I don't feel complete."
"Do you think we'll ever return here?"
"I believe we'll only discover a closing door."
"So, life won't return anywhere near?"
"Not with the way we always end in war."
A whoosh sounded, two children looking up at the end of their lives.

The heat wave came first, melting their skin and removing all but their bones.

As the skeletons fell to the grass in a jumbled mix, the explosions continued across the sky.

*

"Lizzie, that's what you dream of?"

"Every night."

"Do you know who the boy and girl are?"

"Yes and no."

"Do you believe dreams are symbolic? Do you think this dream you continue to have is your stress towards having to leave the only world you've ever known?"

"No. I think I'm dreaming of the end of the world. Of what happened down *there* and forced us to flee up here."

"I see. Well, let's swing back. Who're the boy and girl?"

"Depends."

"On what?"

"On each dream."

"How so?"

"In some it's me and Savannah. In others me and Eric."

"Interesting. Well, here's my second question for you. Do you know *who* you are, Lizzie?"

"Yes and no."

"If I asked you to describe yourself, what would you say?"

"That I'm a ghost within some darkened clouds."

"Is that what you think I see, when I look at you?"

"No, I think you see a soul without a home. A body without a tenant."

"But you have feelings. Thoughts. Empathy. Desire. Surely a ghost or a soulless human wouldn't possess such processes?"

"There's something that's in my mind. It's killing me, Dr. Light. I'm not free, I'm not happy. I don't have hope. I have pain and loneliness. Sadness. I'm lost and I won't find my way. I have no home. No family. And tomorrow... tomorrow I get to jump out of the only place I know and hope that I see my orb, catch it, and a future I want to experience is absorbed from within. I'm tired, I'm young, I'm old and I'm honestly done with the questions."

Dr. Light smiled, setting down her notepad and holding up a finger, indicating for Lizzie to wait one moment. Then she walked off screen.

Lizzie felt a click, and the VR set released. The door opened behind the chair. Looking, Lizzie saw Dr. Light step into the room. She approached, waited for Lizzie to stand, and then they were hugging.

Lizzie felt Dr. Light's sobs first, surprised that the doctor was crying.

"I'll fix myself," Lizzie whispered into her ear.

Dr. Light nodded, stepped back, and wiped her tears dry.

"Lizzie. I wish you didn't have to jump. I do hope you catch your orb. And if you should miss, enjoy the journey after."

They gave a professional handshake, one that affirmed they'd never see each other again, before Dr. Light left the room and Lizzie felt the impending weight of the jump crush them internally.

15.

Lizzie found Savannah waiting at the elevator.

It was unexpected and exactly what was needed.

A moment of recognition before they ran to each other, hugged and kissed.

"I've missed you so much, Lizzie," Savannah said, burying her face in Lizzie's neck.

"Me too," Lizzie replied, inhaling the smell of Savannah's hair as deeply as possible.

"You got selected," Savannah finally said, once they'd stepped apart and stood holding hands.

"I did. I'm so sorry."

"Don't be. It's a truly magical thing to experience."

"My debriefing doctor, Dr. Light, said that now that I'm leaving, your mom gets to move up to the Royal Level. Do you as well?"

"I do."

"That is amazing. I'm so happy for you."

Savannah smiled, her eyes squinting just a touch, filling Lizzie with so much joy that it came as a surprise. Lizzie hadn't felt anything close to that in years.

"I wish we had the rest of our lives together," Savannah said.

"We do," Lizzie replied.

"I don't mean like that," Savannah said, grabbing Lizzie's hips and pulling their bodies together. Her lips found Lizzie's again.

"Will you watch me jump?" Lizzie asked.

"If you want, yes."

"I would."

"Then I will."

"Thank you."

"I love you, Lizzie."

"I love you too."

They remained silent, their fingers dancing over each other's knuckles, feeling each crease.

Lizzie would need to leave soon and get bloodwork done.

Until then, they had the rest of their lives to live.

16. Blood Work

Upon arrival at the Health and Laboratory Level, Lizzie was still buzzing from seeing Savannah.

It was a revelation.

A clinician signed Lizzie in, mentioned they'd been expecting them for blood work. Lizzie was led down another emotionless hallway, into a sterile room filled with stations. The clinician directed Lizzie to sit in one of the cubicles and indicated a nurse would be along shortly.

Lizzie found the room to be dead silent. No buzzing, hissing, or any random noises.

The stillness was interrupted by the soft taps of shoes approaching.

The nurse smiled robotically and asked Lizzie to please reveal an elbow, at which time a metallic clamp extended from the rail and Lizzie's arm was fastened in place.

A needle was inserted, vial after vial of dark red fluid pumping forth. After what seemed like ages, the nurse took a small device from her pocket, placed it to the insertion hole where the blood had been drawn and squeezed. Lizzie smelled the distinct smell of burning flesh, the spot cauterized.

"You may return to your level," the nurse said, walking briskly away.

"I don't have a level," Lizzie called out after them, but received no response.

"Well, fuck."

Lizzie retraced the steps necessary to exit the level, breathing easier once in the elevator.

Unsure where to go, Lizzie pressed the button for the Dormitory Level, hoping to bump into Eric.

Travelling down the levels, a million thoughts flooded through Lizzie's head, but the dream that continued to visit each night was front and center. The kids, the serene beauty of the world, the trails of smoke travelling behind the bombs that went up and up and up.

Before they exploded, the elevator stopped and the door opened. Stepping out, a shudder rolled across Lizzie's body.

The nano-bots were hard at work here, hard at work dismantling the level for repurposing.

17.

Lizzie wasn't sure why it had never occurred to them on the way to the Dormitory Level. The same thing had happened with the High Level and the house. The class had been selected, the area would need to be cleansed and returned to a pristine, untouched living space.

One not tainted by the recently departed.

Lizzie was lost as to what to do now. There had been no instructions on pre-jump protocols or expectations. Were they all supposed to return to the simulator? Was there a special level for them to sleep peacefully one last time before leaping from the ship?

An idea struck, one that seemed foolish but also possible.

Returning to the elevator, Lizzie popped the panel down that was hidden beside the buttons. Royals and High Level citizens knew of this access panel, but it wasn't something that was shared.

Lizzie pushed the call button, a chime sounded and a woman spoke.

"How may I be of assistance?"

"I've been selected for Salvation and I jump tomorrow. My home has been dismantled and the

Dormitory Level is currently being repurposed. Where am I supposed to go?"

A chime sounded again, the woman replied.

"Students chosen for Salvation will receive instructions at the Jump Level. I will transport you there now. Be warned, it is the lowest level of the ship, the descent can be unsettling."

"Thank you."

"Please, pop the access panel back into place and hang on."

Lizzie did as instructed. Once it clicked into the spot, Lizzie grasped the rail and braced.

The elevator plunged down, feeling as though it had failed and that it would crash through the bottom of the shaft and eject both occupant and car into space.

After an agonizingly long drop, the car gradually slowed until Lizzie no longer worried about an imminent death. Soon, it came to a halt. The door opened and Lizzie stepped out into a mixture of nervous banter, excited movement, and faces flooded with emotion.

"Ah, Lizzie, there you are. Now we can go over the last bit of preparation and you can all go eat and have a relaxing night before the big day tomorrow."

The man clapped his hands and motioned for the students to follow. Lizzie recognized them all with varying degrees. Some had shaved their heads for a better fit in their helmets, others hadn't shaved their faces since selection day, scruffy beards aging them. All in all, the group of students were about to go through the same experience. They'd all step to the edge, receive one last instruction, and then leap through the stratosphere, looking for their orb.

They entered a smaller room, old wooden benches lining the walls. It was clear that this space wasn't used often, and with it being a place only utilized before a group of students was about to jump, it didn't need to be fancy or comfortable.

"Everyone, settle. Thank you. My name is Jack Eldridge. You may recognize the last name. I *am* a Royal, a descendant of Mr. Eldridge himself, the creator of Empyrean. I have the privilege of going through the final preparations with you for your big day, and I will be there tomorrow to help you jump."

A palpable energy emitted from the group, the celebrity worship of a living and breathing Eldridge before them making the rounds.

"Tomorrow will be the single greatest moment of each of your lives. In the morning, you will wake up, finding breakfast will be waiting. Eat. Shower. Take a moment to reflect individually about what being selected for Salvation means to you. A chime will sound, similar to this one," he pushed a small black device in his hand, a chime emanating, "at which point you will make your way here. Once you arrive, each of you will have a team to help you suit up, check your helmet and then direct you into the jumping order. It has been randomly chosen. I know you are excited, scared, unsure, nervous, so many things. But, I want to assure you, the hardest part will be the leap tomorrow."

"What if we can't jump?"

For a second Lizzie believed they'd asked the question, as it was on the tip of their tongue, but then realized it was from a sheepish boy huddled in the far corner. The color of his face and the sweat on his forehead suggested he was moments from puking.

"Salvation is mandatory. You have been specifically selected by Mr. Eldridge himself so that each of you will achieve your futures. I don't want to alarm you or upset you, but once at the edge, you can jump. Or if not, we have steps in place to ensure you leave the platform."

"You'll push us?" the boy asked.

"No, no. I assure you not. Much like the simulations, a countdown will sound, a jump alarm will alert you that it is time to jump. If you do not jump within five seconds, the section of platform you are standing on will unhinge and you will find yourself in free fall. We only have so much time available for you all to jump. Due to the Earth's rotation, the ship's revolutions, and the area that the orbs ascend, we need to stay on schedule."

That revelation dropped the excitement by a few notches in the room, as they all grasped the reality of what was to happen tomorrow. It was no longer a *thing*, an event, it was something that had to happen and would, by any means necessary.

"Alright, if there's no more questions," he pointed at the first six students sitting to his left, "you six can come with me. I'll lead you through the walk up ramp, the platform, and then you are free to head to the cafeteria. Eat, head to your assigned room for the evening, and try to get some rest. Tomorrow is a big day. For you and for the ship."

The first six shuffled off after the man, leaving the rest to sit in stunned silence.

Lizzie had expected hushed conversations to begin, but instead everyone had their heads bowed, eyes at the floor. It was only then that Lizzie realized Eric was not in the room.

18.

A thousand questions rapidly flooded Lizzie's brain as the search for Eric began.

Taking their time, Lizzie looked at each and every student sitting in the room, not expecting to find him but hoping he would be sitting there. Why he wouldn't be sitting beside Lizzie was unknown, but when his face wasn't spotted, a more alarming question fired off inside; *where exactly was he?*

They were a tandem, selected to jump together. Now, on the night before the big day, Eric wasn't here? Lizzie was surprised to feel a sting of hurt, a burning pain that forced itself beside the rising anger.

"Excuse me?"

Nobody noticed, nor pretended to care.

"Excuse me?" Lizzie said louder, getting the attention of the lady who'd been standing near Jack Eldridge.

"Yes?"

"My jump partner, Eric. He's not here."

"He should be. You were the last student we were waiting on. One moment, let me check."

The lady left the room. Once gone the hushed conversations now started, some of the students glancing over at Lizzie and away again when they saw a returned glare.

The lady returned with Eric walking behind her. He didn't look well. His face was a match for the boy in the corner.

"Are you OK?" Lizzie asked.

"I'm not doing so well. Think nerves. Sorry, I had to rush off. I didn't want to vomit on anyone."

Lizzie started laughing. At first it was a low giggle before it transformed into full on howling.

"What's so funny?" Eric asked, appearing angry.

"I just can't believe you, of all people, were nervous and threw up."

Eric chuckled a bit now, the queasiness preventing a full laugh.

"Sure, laugh it up."

They bumped shoulders, Lizzie feeling a sense of security that he was in fact here. They kept giggling about Eric's state until they were summoned.

*

Lizzie took Eric's hand as they waited for the pair before them to finish.

Once Jack Eldridge waved them up, Lizzie found an unexpected anxiety rushing forth. Eric was breathing heavy, confirming he felt the same.

"Greetings. Lizzie, Eric," Jack said, nodding as the two stepped onto the platform.

"OK. Tomorrow, big day, big day, big day," he said, excitedly rubbing his hands together. Lizzie noticed his nails were uncut, long. Dirt was crusted around them, which caused a repulsed response. "Now, let me look at you two. This'll never do." He sized up Lizzie, examined Eric.

"Hmm, I think we need you on this side, Eric," Jack pushed Eric from Lizzie's right to Lizzie's left.

"Perfect!" He clapped his hands and smiled, a level of derangement becoming exposed.

"Before we begin, do you have any questions?"

Eric looked at Lizzie expecting something. Lizzie remained quiet, so Eric took the initiative.

"What happens if we miss our orb?"

Jack smiled, an unhinged flash of energy darting across his eyes.

"Excellent question. Do you know what happens when you catch your orb?"

"We absorb our future."

"COOOORRECT!" Jack's reply caused Lizzie's knees to almost buckle. This was a madman made up to resemble a leader. He rapidly licked his lips.

"And if we miss?" Eric was trying not to sound frustrated, but Jack was deflecting and Lizzie could see Eric's temper being tested.

"Did you know that I've jumped?"

Lizzie and Eric both snapped to attention at what Jack said.

"You... jumped? But how are you here?"

"It's true. When I was your age, I was selected. SALVATION. I jumped. The future I absorbed was for me to be onboard the revolving ship. VOILA!"

Lizzie wasn't sure if he was being sarcastic, but it was becoming incredibly hard to take him seriously.

"Are you a Returner?" Lizzie asked.

Jack's smile immediately disappeared.

"Who told you about that?"

"Dr. Light. In debriefing."

Jack's smile returned, his eyes boring holes into Lizzie.

"Back on task then? Yeah? We have a batch of nervous jumpers behind you."

"Sure," they both said, wanting to get it over and done with.

"So, tomorrow, the countdown starts," he pointed at the square LCD screen on the wall. Much to Lizzie and Eric's surprise, the number twenty became visible and began to count down. "Don't worry, this is just a visual representation so you know where to look."

Lizzie didn't feel comforted.

"You two will stand right here. See the markings here and here," he pointed, Lizzie noted again how long his nails were. Something about that was unexpectedly disturbing. Royals were privileged. Clean. "When the jump signal sounds, it is just like the simulator all over again. Take a breath, bend at the knees and then leap out as far as you can. From there, I wish you the greatest joy and most amazing future your orb can ever deliver."

Lizzie looked at the timer, finding it had stopped at five seconds.

"OK, you two. I'll see you tomorrow. NEXT!"

Jack had already motioned for the next two to step to the platform, forcing Lizzie and Eric to leave and make their way through the side door, down a short hallway which brought them to the entrance of the cafeteria.

"Are you even hungry?" Lizzie asked.

"Not really, but after throwing up everything I've ever ingested, I probably should eat," Eric replied, offering up a laugh to try and convince Lizzie he was joking.

"Fine, let's grab something and get this over with. I want to try to get some sleep."

Eric followed Lizzie to the line of people holding trays, waiting for food.

They walked along as the line moved, having various items spooned onto their plate. A last supper for those making their last walk.

They dined in silence, the clanging of silverware the only sound.

Once done, the scrape of chair legs on the floor signalled the herd leaving for their rooms.

For some the night would last forever, their brains excitedly keeping them awake.

For others, they'd be asleep before they were fully under the covers, one last glimpse of the stars winking at them far off in the universe.

Eric wished Lizzie a good night, before stepping into his room and closing the door.

Lizzie found their assigned room right beside Eric's. The interior was stark and plain, nothing fancy needed for someone who wouldn't even reside on the ship in twenty four hours' time.

Lizzie pulled a stool over before the window and sat, watching the Earth share the last of its beauty.

When the eyes grew heavy, the body followed, making it to the bed and pulling the covers.

Lizzie wasn't sure what tomorrow would bring, what the jump would be like, but one thing that was for sure; Lizzie would be having a familiar dream.

19.

*

The girl woke first, spotting the boy still sleeping in his bed.

"Wake up," she said, tossing some stuffed animals towards him.

"What time is it?"

"Morning!"

They scrambled forth, two balls of energy in pajamas.

Running around the room, they pushed, pulled and tackled each other. Finally spent, they kneeled on the boy's bed, looking outside, wondering what type of weather they'd been given that day.

Seeing the sun shining down on the lush green grass, they squealed in delight and leapt from the bed.

Barely a sole touched the floor as they sprinted out into the wide open space. They pushed, pulled and tackled each other, rolling in the sand and the grass. Laughing and yelling, they found the swings, the slides and monkey bars.

It was the boy who spotted the trails in the sky first.

"What's that?"

"Dunno."

The boy noticed the odd screen hanging from a tree, the numbers displayed counting down.

"What's that?"

"Dunno."

Above them, more trails filled the sky, more moments stolen from a future that would never be.

They returned to the swings, propelling themselves higher and higher.

The clock in the tree counted lower and lower.

As the boy and girl ascended to the apex of their flight path, the clock struck zero, the sky flashed bright orange and the sound of a million souls screamed as everything evaporated in the blink of an eye.

*

20.

Lizzie awoke covered in sweat and breathing hard.

Looking around the darkened room, a sense of calm descended, finding a room instead of the remains of a scorched earth.

Locating the side table clock, Lizzie let out a sigh. As always, the alarm was going to sound in two minutes.

No extra sleep this time. No extra sleep ever again.

It was jump day.

Lizzie stood, stretched and tried to suffocate the giant ball of dread that sat on the space normally reserved for a heart.

What was to come?

Nobody knew for sure.

The only certainty was Lizzie would no longer be calling the revolving ship home, and in only a few hours an orb would be the only thing that mattered.

21. JUMP

Lizzie walked into the cafeteria for the last breakfast.

It all felt surreal, as though the students were walking in a cloud, the edges fuzzy and blurry, the painting unfinished.

"Lizzie," Eric called out, waving. "I already grabbed you some food."

Lizzie found Eric had loaded up two plates with a selection of everything on offer.

"I didn't know what you'd want, so take what you'd like."

He was shovelling forkful after forkful of food in his mouth. Lizzie was surprised he didn't choke.

"How are you?"

"I don't know. You?"

"Beyond excited. I think yesterday's anxiety has left and I'm just pumped to jump," Eric said, taking another massive bite of food.

"That's great."

"Have you thought about what it's going to feel like? We've obviously experienced the rush of grabbing the orbs in the simulator, but this... this is *for real.*"

Lizzie chuckled at Eric's enthusiasm. It was refreshing that he felt this way, lowering the uncertainty and unease that Lizzie was experiencing.

"Thirty minutes," a woman called out from the side of the room. Lizzie looked over, not having noticed her before. She was dressed in a standard Empyrean uniform, but she wasn't one of the women who'd assisted Jack Eldridge the previous day.

With the announcement, the peripheral noise increased as students ate faster, and conversations picked up.

Lizzie took time eating a muffin. It wasn't particularly good, but it was the only thing that enticed the hungry jumper.

"You wanna go to the pre-jump area and just have some quiet?"

Lizzie looked at Eric, thankful for the suggestion.

"Yes. That would be wonderful."

They placed their plates and utensils in the collection bin, and left the still gorging students.

22.

"I want you to know that I really do love you."

Lizzie looked at Eric, who nodded.

"I don't want you to think I'm only saying it because we're about to jump."

"Oh, Lizzie. I'd never think that."

"My heart has always been locked. You were the key."

Lizzie placed a hand against his chest, leaned in and kissed him. It was a quick, gentle, emotion-filled kiss. Enough to share their feelings and say their goodbyes.

The sounds of approaching students forced them to step away from each other. They hurried ahead, finding their assigned spot.

Once they sat, the process began.

Their assistant came and fitted them with their jumpsuits. They were thinner and tighter than the simulator suits. When Eric lifted his arms up from his sides, thin, membranous wings unfolded.

"Neat."

Next the assistant aided their boot selection. They were also snug and light. Lizzie wasn't sure why, but the cushioning and tread on the bottom was better than expected, an odd detail that stuck in the mind. The gloves were better than the simulator gloves,

Lizzie happy to see how well these ones fit each finger. The simulator ones had to fit everyone, which typically left an inch of loose material when Lizzie wore them.

Last was the helmet. Significantly lighter and more aerodynamic than the simulator helmets, Lizzie found once the helmet was clipped in place it was still possible to breathe. The visor wasn't fogging up, and it wasn't pressing hard into Lizzie's nose or jaw.

"Look at this," Eric said, visor retracted. "Wish the simulator ones did this."

"No expense spared for the ones about to be eliminated."

"Now, Lizzie. Come on. This is a big deal. People from the ship will be watching from the Observation Level. This is important."

Lizzie had forgotten about that part.

Savannah would be watching.

The Observation Level was two above where they were now, overhanging enough so that the ones who came to watch would be able to see the jumpers' descent until the orbs arrived.

A rush of feelings came with the thought of Savannah watching. Lizzie missed her dearly, but was comforted with Eric as their jump partner. It was a different love for Savannah than for Eric. If Lizzie was forced to choose, it would be impossible.

"T-minus five minutes," a robotic voice sounded from a hidden speaker in the room.

That's when it hit. This was happening. The mood in the room deflated, and all of the students understood that in less than five minutes, they'd be forever leaving the place they'd always called home.

Last second checks were done on all of the jump suits. Clips tightened, zippers zipped, shoulders patted, good lucks wished.

When the voice came back on to announce the first students were to report to the platform, it was as though time had sped up.

Assistants hustled, getting the students into their respective jump order.

Lizzie knew there was no going back from here. Breathing changed, vision blurred on the periphery, the room grew brighter. Eric put one hand on their shoulder, squeezing with some encouragement. Lizzie hadn't considered this moment to mean all that much, but now that it was happening, it meant so much and more.

What would the orb hold? What was the future that was to come? The possibilities were endless and unlimited. All of the worlds wide open, shining and sparkling like broken glass shimmering underneath lights in the dark.

"When I got out of bed today, I swear I didn't think any of this was real," Lizzie whispered to Eric. "I have no idea where my body will go. But, I hope wherever my soul ends up, it ends up with you."

Eric looked into Lizzie's eyes and smiled. His own shone with the wetness of tears. This was their goodbye. Their time together on this plain was over. With the helmets on, they couldn't kiss. So, he leaned forward and gave Lizzie's helmet a gentle tap with his own. Then he flipped his own visor down and took Lizzie's hand, wrapping their fingers together.

They were up next, the line progressing. They watched as two students stepped into place. Jack spoke to them, the deafening roar of open space not letting his words carry back to Eric and Lizzie. The countdown started, came to zero, and the students jumped.

The timer reset, Jack looked over and waved to them.

It was their turn now.

23.

*

"Do you feel alive?

"I do."

"Are we going to spend the rest of our lives together?"

"I wish we could. But I don't think that's something that can happen."

"Why's that?"

"Because of that," the girl said to the boy, pointing as the sky grew red and the heat rushed forward.

*

24.

As proud as they could, they walked to the platform, looking at Jack, glad that the visors didn't allow for direct eye contact.

"You two ready?" he yelled.

The opening before them was the single most intimidating thing they'd ever seen.

Open space.

The sound that greeted them was reminiscent of a symphony coming into key and time together. A jumbled mixture of loud with soft running between the strings.

Lizzie braced on the platform. While the level was pressurized, the vacuum of space still worked to pull anything not bolted down out of the ship, out into the vastness of its clutches.

"Start the timer!"

The screen blinked into life and started to count down.

"Eric. Lizzie. We from Empyrean wish you the greatest of futures to come. Thank you for your contributions to our society. May you find peace and whatever your heart desires."

Eric squeezed Lizzie's hand, Lizzie squeezed back.

"You may jump in... three... two... one... GO!"

They lowered, legs coiled and feet pressing firmly against the surface of the ship.

Then, with one explosive push, they jumped, leaping towards open space and the final free fall of their lives.

25.

The first thousand feet was silent.

Beautiful.

The atmospheric changes between space and the Earth created a crystal effect. Purples and blues and greens danced through Lizzie's eyes. A kaleidoscope of infinite variations.

If Lizzie could, they would've turned and looked back once more at the ship, watched it grow smaller. One last attempt to catch a glimpse of Savannah.

Would she miss me?

The force applied to the jumpers didn't allow for this, so instead Lizzie focused on getting into the correct position and searching for the orbs that would begin to float towards them.

Lizzie realized they were still holding hands with Eric.

Below them, the green and blue of the land mass was all they could see. Lizzie squeezed Eric's hand once more and let go.

Their partnership had reached the very end, for as long as they could stay together.

Now, in free fall as an individual, Lizzie began to seek any sign of the orbs.

Off on the peripheral left, something flickered. Moving only their eyes, Lizzie saw a group of orbs rapidly approaching Eric. He was going to achieve his dream first and Lizzie was going to be able to watch.

A flood of wonder washed throughout as the orbs grew in size and number. Lizzie took a few more looks to see if any were coming towards them, but as of yet, none.

Lizzie watched as Eric spread his arms, zoned in on a cherry colored orb and prepared for contact. If Lizzie could've seen his face, they were positive Eric would be smiling.

As the orbs neared Eric, Lizzie found the sound of space was growing in volume. The helmet was doing a great job of dampening the noise, but a rumble of discomfort was forming deep in the brain.

The sound became unbearable as Eric was one hundred feet away. Travelling at the speed they were, it was a blink of the eye and Eric crashed full on into the cherry red orb. Lizzie saw a moment of blinding light, and then... Eric and the orb disappeared. Lizzie let out a hitch, a sob stuck deep in the throat, as Eric was taken and removed forever from their former shared world.

There was no time to mourn Eric, as Lizzie was still catapulting towards Earth, travelling faster and faster.

A new thought started to fester. Previously the worry had been about not catching the orb. Now, only one thought sat at the forefront of all the others.

What if no orbs come?

Pushing the thought away, Lizzie followed protocol, getting their arms and legs positioned correctly.

Come on orbs, where are you?

The Earth continued to grow in size, the space between the jumper and the surface becoming smaller and smaller.

Then.

Then, little dots far below. They started to grow, larger and larger until Lizzie practically shouted inside the helmet.

Orbs!

Lizzie pushed out every other thought that tried to interfere. This was no simulation, this was the real deal. Failure here would be catastrophic.

The balls of light danced and wavered, approaching Lizzie as though unsure what was hurtling through space in their direction.

Lizzie realized a smile was plastered across their face, suddenly excited about what may become possible with the arrival of the orbs.

They flickered and shimmered, colors morphing as though playing a game with the perspective person.

Lizzie tried to track down the orb just for them. In the simulation the color had been obvious, but as their instructors had said time and time again, *'during the jump, your orb will be just for* you, *so watch for the one that means the most.*

Lizzie kept those words solidly at the front, pushing back every other memory and distraction that tried to wiggle its way around it.

The one that means the most, the one that means the most, Lizzie told themselves over and over.

The orbs were closer, the Earth was nearer and nothing was coming to Lizzie. Panic set in, anxiety trying to move vomit from the stomach to the mouth, but with the helmet on that wasn't an option.

Lizzie gulped it back down, blinking and trying to clear their vision.

There it is.

Between the reds and blues and oranges, the orb that would mean the most singled itself out from the rest. Lizzie couldn't believe it.

Instead of a solid color, or a glowing sphere, Lizzie's orb was a scaled down version of the Earth and it was speeding directly towards them.

Now, all Lizzie needed to do was catch it.

26.

The Earth-orb spun around and around, the outlines of each continent highlighted by the dark blues of each ocean.

Lizzie hoped that absorption would mean being reunited. With Mom. With Eric and Savannah. With some semblance of normality.

The orb was only one hundred feet away.

Seventy five.

Lizzie's life flashed through their mind.

The sorrow of the Warding Level.

Adoption.

Moments of pure joy, extreme sadness, mixed between blitzes of laughter and anger.

Mom's last breath. Lizzie's pained howls as they laid in the bed with the deceased.

Fifty feet.

Twenty five.

Arms stretched wide. Legs positioned for the optimum angular chance.

Lizzie had never felt anything like this. No experience had ever come close to the realization that the orb was directly before them, the Earth shining bright with every single moment of the rest of their lives seconds from being caught and absorbed.

Every hope, want and dream about to become a reality.

Was this what Eric had experienced?

AND THEN.

Lizzie blasted into the orb, the entire spectrum of the universe illuminating and osmotically travelling from the skin of the sphere, across the synapses and deep into Lizzie's brain.

The noise that erupted within caused both ear drums to scream and pop, which created a muted, dull hum. Lizzie was surprised to not feel any panic. Instead, Lizzie realized that the orb was still within their arms and the immense, real Earth was approaching at a far greater speed than before.

Lizzie screamed at the top of their lungs, holding tight the glowing globe within their arms as the first hints of flames from re-entry began to form and swallow the human and the ball in a self-contained burning prison.

*

'Do you think it'll hurt when we burn?'

'I don't think we'll feel anything.'

'I can feel the air getting hotter and my skin starting to bubble.'

'I'm sorry that this is the end.'

'Don't be. I'd rather die having known you, than live without ever having met you.'

'That's very kind.'

'I mean it.'

*

No pain was felt.

Lizzie continued to accelerate towards the surface of the abandoned planet, gripping the orb as tightly as they could.

When they were only a few miles above the surface, Lizzie braced for impact, expecting a cataclysmic explosion to occur on arrival.

Much to their surprise, everything went black a few feet from the ground, the flames having long ago burned themselves out.

27. Earth

Returning to consciousness on the scalding pavement, Lizzie rolled over and rushed onto the grass. The simmering ash remains of their orb were plastered on the cement where they'd crashed to the surface. As Lizzie looked at the place of impact where obsidian specks of pavement popped and sputtered before sizzling until quiet.

Looking skyward, Lizzie watched. It was speckled with orbs travelling from the planet, heading towards the jumpers. Every so often a small flash would occur, the meaning not lost. Those were the successful absorbers, something Lizzie was not.

Don't cry, Savannah's voice said, filling Lizzie's mind with hope.

Looking again, Lizzie could see a larger shining object beyond the orbs. The revolving ship. Former home. It was such a strange thing to look up at and realize that Lizzie was now standing on the planet they'd looked at lovingly for almost two decades.

Are you hurt?

Now it was Eric's voice talking inside Lizzie's head. Friends were forever.

"No."

Good. You need to walk. Do you see where the orbs are coming from? People are there. Your future awaits.

Lizzie nodded, heading towards where the orbs were originating from. They had no idea what would be waiting for them, but walking under the open space being filled with the futures of so many young people gave buoyancy to the hope that a place for Lizzie now and for the rest of time would be waiting.

As they started to walk another orb rocketed up into the atmosphere.

28.

Nothing had ever prepared Lizzie for the dread induced feeling of walking on the planet. Animals made noises and scurried around, the wind picked up, smells assaulted Lizzie's nose. Under the open sky, with no walls as boundaries and no windows showing the Earth beyond it, Lizzie felt nauseous and frightened, as though a single step would cause them to be propelled from the grass that lined the side of the cement path that they were following.

I thought this planet was void of life?

The thought kept nagging at Lizzie.

Whenever anything made a noise or moved off in the trees or bushes, Lizzie immediately panicked and had to work as hard as they could to not take off running, afraid of what might happen were they to do so.

Instead, Lizzie steeled their resolve and confidently walked towards the location of the orbs.

Sensation overload reared time and time again. The beating sun, the lush breeze, the uneven surface. Simply walking in this new world was a brand new experience that tested Lizzie's body in strange ways. And while Lizzie had experienced the Empyrean designed-and-created sun and wind before, this was completely different. Real.

The cement pathway, which was as wide as any hallway Lizzie had been in, travelled further ahead, before disappearing up a hill into the trees. Lizzie knew it would lead them to their destination.

The middle of the pathway had faded markings on it. Thinking through some of the lessons Lizzie could remember, this must have been something called a highway. The markings were placed to separate the users moving back and forth in opposite directions. It was during this thought that Lizzie spotted a large metallic object on the side of the cement path. It was scorched and hollowed out.

Approaching it, Lizzie recognized the body of what used to be a car. Looking around, they could see the remnants of burn marks through the trees around the area. A strange calm arrived, Lizzie sensing a familiarity that shouldn't be there.

Continuing to walk along the side of the forgotten highway, Lizzie arrived at the base of the hill. Still above, the orbs soared and popped. How many more jumpers were there? Lizzie was unsure. Surely, their class wasn't the only group selected? Forced was more accurate. What was even true anymore?

A new noise stole Lizzie's attention. A babbling brook, just over the edge of the grassy area. Realizing just how thirsty they were, Lizzie hopped down and landed on the soft dirt by the water. Kneeling, Lizzie cupped their hands and grimaced as the ice cold water filled their mouth. This might've been the coldest drink they'd ever had.

It tasted divine.

Lizzie cupped mouthful after mouthful of the sublime drink. Finally, their stomach filled, Lizzie stopped, feeling content and ready to attack the final stretch of the path ahead.

Returning to the cement roadway, Lizzie was glad to continue walking.

Up the hill, into the trees, the view started to change. At first all Lizzie could see were more trees and the cement line that cut through the middle. Further along, it adjusted, the hills further apart, the trees moving away from the edges.

Lizzie couldn't believe it. When they'd lived on the revolving ship the Earth had looked like such a distant thing, as though its textures and intricacies were flat and one dimensional.

Now, standing at the crest of the hill, looking down over the valley before them, Lizzie was stunned. The shapes and sizes of what could be seen was momentous. A painting come to life. School lessons leaping from the class to stand right before them.

A body of water connected to a white sand beach. A small village beyond and the mountains acted as a picturesque backdrop.

This was everything Lizzie had ever believed the Earth would truly look like.

A sudden primal urge to strip nude and sprint into the water overcame Lizzie. To feel the sand beneath the feet, the body slicing through the water and the sky as the only thing looking down was an intoxicating idea.

But Lizzie pushed it away.

Lizzie walked into the town.

The streets were empty.

No movement ahead or on either side. Lizzie approached with hesitance, looking for anything, still unsure of their place in this world.

The town had been abandoned and discarded, long forgotten by those who might've once cared or resided here.

As Lizzie came to its main street, the intersection filled them with sadness over what had become.

Was Eldridge and Empyrean responsible for all of this?

Was this what became of the world when the bombs exploded and those living on the ship ignored the place below them? The people left behind?

Every teacher, every piece of information had stated that the Earth was no more, that the remnants of the former human civilization had been reclaimed by the land. Even during debriefing that had been what Lizzie was told. But it wasn't true.

Doors and windows were boarded up. Any window that had been left exposed had been shattered and broken, some of the remnants still laying on the sidewalk. Behind the dark opening, Lizzie could see shelves with products, a thick layer of dust covering those cans or knick-knacks closest to the street. They knew that any memories that might still float in the space beyond the black had long since packed their bags and moved on, hoping to find greener pastures.

Lizzie could see the inviting beach and water ahead, appearing and disappearing between each building. The town skyline, minor as it was, made for an animated puzzle that had scattered pieces missing throughout.

These had been people's livelihoods. Their jobs. Their hopes and dreams, created from and within these places.

A bitter taste formed in Lizzie's mouth.

While residents lived aboard the ship, the Earth's survivors down here had struggled, been discarded, and practically starved to death. Mr. Eldridge didn't care. All he cared about was his survival, his prosperity.

Hell, Eldridge had fled the Earth when the world's grid had collapsed, and while Lizzie had long been told that he was a savior of the people by creating and taking in people on his revolving ship, the truth was he was a coward. The Returners knew about how things were down here. This fact made Lizzie incredibly angry.

More hunks of metal appeared as Lizzie came to a four-way stop. The red octagon faded and dented, left to rot on the metal stem that held it in place. Something caught Lizzie's eye. They walked over to the shape, kneeling to inspect what turned out to be the skeleton of a deceased animal. Tiny tufts of hair still held firm on a few of the bleached white bones, the long tail suggesting this had been a cat. Tears welled up in Lizzie's eyes, a mixture of emotions surging forth with each grim new discovery. Part of the emotion, Lizzie realized, was that the cat hadn't died all that long ago. The Empyrean lie was beginning to cause stabbing pains where Lizzie felt them the most – the soul.

Leaving the remains behind, a noise was the next thing to get Lizzie's attention. Looking around, they found the source was a black wire that hung lax between two wooden poles. The purpose of the wire was unknown, but as Lizzie looked further, they could see that the wires travelled off in all directions between more and more of the tall poles. Some were standing straight up and down, while others had dangerous leans to them.

As Lizzie continued on, they found the street was beginning to slope. Making their way down the decline, a complete despondency overcame them. Here were overgrown yards, rusted tricycles and shuttered houses. All life that had called these dwellings home had ended, all color and joy sucked out in an instance, left to rot abandoned and in ruin until the Earth itself reclaimed the space.

Lizzie's presence was that of a ghost without a home. A feeling they'd experienced their entire life now became the reality. Something shared with Dr. Light, now right before them in the here and now. Each footstep that carried them forward was another step of a being walking through a world that had long ago left them behind. *Maybe, I did catch my orb*, Lizzie thought. *Maybe I'm meant to be alone and to feel meaningless and inconsequential forever?*

Scorch marks and ash were the only signs of what had created the town's pain. A series of familiar-shaped silhouettes along a broken and partially crumbled cement wall forced Lizzie to stop, a hand going to their mouth to halt a cry. The final farewell. A blackened photo of the outline of people, snuffed out in an instant.

A change of surface alerted Lizzie to just where they'd ended up. They were now standing at the beginning of the sandy beach. The sun beat down, the water lapped at the shore. The moment was perfect, clear, and such a difference in scenery and atmosphere from what lay just behind Lizzie that they struggled to connect what was before them.

They walked over to the dock that led to water that travelled to the edge of the horizon. Sitting on the dock cross-legged, Lizzie looked down into the clear, calm water.

How deep was it? Did any animals still live below the surface?

Lizzie turned their gaze skyward. Searching for any sign of the ship.

Was Savannah ok? Had she moved to the Royal Level?

The fact so many people had lied to Lizzie, to the students, and had done for so many years, stung.

Lizzie missed the old view, the one that looked down on the Earth, back when things had been simpler. Back before they knew the truth.

Now, sitting here, looking at the heavens, Lizzie felt discarded, as though their existence alone was an inconvenience worthy of forcing them out, forcing them to jump. Eldridge had said their selection was chosen, not random. That made the deception even more frustrating.

Lizzie had always asked what would happen if they missed their orb, didn't catch it. But Lizzie should've asked what life was like on Earth. Were there survivors down here? It didn't look like there were. But this was only one small place on a massive spinning globe.

Once again, Lizzie was living but feeling nothing. The emotions that should be waging a battle beneath the surface were being pushed further away as they walked through the exact situation Lizzie found themselves in.

The life up there was over.

The life down here was Lizzie's reality.

They'd jumped and not been absorbed.

Lizzie's mom had been right. Lizzie was special.

The thought of their mom's constant encouragement was the kick they needed. Lizzie wouldn't allow themselves to become a Ward of this planet.

They had lived. Survived.

Standing, Lizzie took one last look at the water that stretched further away than space ever had.

While they may have initially found themselves lost, Lizzie had now found their way.

Turning, they were surprised to see a blast of orbs fire off into the sky, from far up the hillside in the town. Why hadn't they seen orbs while walking through the town? Was there a cloaking or camouflaging device in place to shield them?

From here, they could see a cylindrical shaped building. It reminded them of the old news stories about Nuclear energy. As Lizzie walked, a noise similar to that of someone strumming a harp sounded, and each time it did, an orb burst from the top of the building and accelerated far up into the stratosphere.

Lizzie had found their destination.

Hurrying, they wanted to get there while the orbs were still launching.

Arriving at the building, Lizzie searched for an entry. It wasn't until the far side of the structure that one was located. Fumbling with the unfamiliar knob, Lizzie got it turned and pulled the door open. Stepping through, a blast of heat greeted Lizzie, making them take a step back. Blinking a few times, they regained their bearings and stepped into the structure.

A device that looked like a massive microscope filled up the center of the space. Beside it, Lizzie spotted two figures frantically scooping material into an opening with shovels. It was bubbling up from a nearby pit, the red glowing bright against the darkness of whatever was within. It spit and hissed with each shovelful, the figures squealing from each splatter. As they scooped, the tube above blazed bright, before the material slithered up the sides. Once it reached the top of the tube, the material was pushed through an opening. Lizzie's eyes went wide, as the material formed into a perfectly shaped orb. The tune of the harp sounded again, someone yelled *'launch!'* and the newly created orb was shot from the structure.

It was then that Lizzie noticed a hunched figure sitting in a chair near the base of the large object that occupied the building. They were intently looking into a viewfinder, tracking the trajectory of each sphere.

Approaching slowly, knowing that when they spoke Lizzie would most likely scare the figures, they took in the outfit the figure was wearing.

White lab coat. Glasses. Bandages criss-crossing their face.

"Excuse me?" Lizzie said, watching as they jumped at the unexpected, intruding voice.

"Who the hell are you?" the figure at the microscope asked, whirling around in their chair.

"I'm Lizzie. Who are you?"

The figure shuffled off the chair, coming towards Lizzie. They were about the same height as Lizzie, but otherwise they were far from what humans looked like on the ship. Male. Emaciated, hairless and eyes bulging behind the lenses, Lizzie was unsure where to look.

"I'm Dr. Harkins. Where did you come from? You are new to me. To *here*." His head bobbed around, inspecting Lizzie up and down, side to side.

"I'm from the ship. I jumped, caught my orb, but instead of being absorbed I landed on Earth."

A shocked gasp came from the three figures as Lizzie shared what had happened.

"The revolving ship? You're a star person?"

"I guess."

"Are you Empyrean scum?"

"Pardon?"

"If you're from where you claim you are, you must be Empyrean scum, yes? Mr. Eldridge work his claws into why *you're* up there and *we're* down here? Scraping and fighting for morsels of uncontaminated food that he sends when the occasion suits him."

"I was a student. Our class was selected to jump for our future."

"Ahh, haha. Yes. The *orbs*. The *future*. Nothing but rubbish. Each orb is filled with my concoction, you see. Molten-acid, I'm afraid. Our way of giving back to the vengeful *God* that lords above us in his ship. In your case, we simply failed. Sadly you lived."

Lizzie's eyes went wide. If that was true, that would mean Eric was gone-gone. That absorption was actually eradication.

"But Jack told me he'd jumped before?"

"Ha! Jack Eldridge?" Dr. Harkins spit a dark-green gob to the floor, where it sizzled upon impact. Wiping some sweat from his forehead, he continued. "He'll say whatever needs to be said to keep his spot on that ship. Such a grotesque thing he is. He delivers our food from time to time. He'll even give us more if we find his addictions for him. Real piece of work, that man."

Lizzie's head spun. Was this all for real? The orbs were supposed to be the answer for them. Their future. The ship was their bastion until selected. From there, everything was preparation for the jump.

Anger grew.

"I can see you're realizing what I've said is true. How you survived, beats me. But you did. You wanted a future. Maybe I can offer one for you?"

Lizzie's eyes flashed with rage at the figure. Whatever was happening here on the surface was taking its toll on the residents.

He stepped towards Lizzie, one of the bandages coming loose, fluttered, exposing the open sores beneath, the charred skin surrounding it. The work they did here was killing them, the random splashes and spills eating them away.

"This can't be true," was all Lizzie could manage.

"My dear, I'm afraid it is. Look around. Look at what man did to this planet. To this town. We fight and we battle for every day of our existence."

"And you would offer me a future?"

"Absolutely."

"Why?"

"Because, you're from up there. You know *things*."

Lizzie thought of the town and what had become of the place. The Earth, in all its beauty, reduced to a wasteland from Eldridge's greed. Lizzie thought of the dreams, the memories, the hope that seemed to dance when this strange little figure spoke of them remaining here and helping them.

"Where do we begin?"

The man smiled, disfigured face sharing happiness in Lizzie's decision.

"I'm so pleased, Lizzie. Come, my new friend. Let's make a place for you. One that will give you everything you always wanted."

Lizzie smiled and followed the doctor, feeling happier than they'd had in some time. The tune of the harp sounded again, another orb rocketing into space.

Heading towards the ship above them, towards an unsuspecting jumper believing that everything they ever wanted was contained in that acid filled sphere.

For some their future was before them when they looked down.

For others, the future was above.

END

To be continued in...
The Bandaged: The Empyrean Saga Book Two

ABOUT THE AUTHOR

Steve Stred is the Splatterpunk Nominated Author of 'Sacrament' and 'Mastodon.'

Based in Edmonton, Alberta, Canada, Steve has released over a dozen novels and novellas as well as a number of collections. He has appeared alongside some of horror's biggest names within some truly excellent anthologies.

He is a proud co-founder of the LOHF Writer's Grant and an Active Member of the HWA.

Website: stevestredauthor.wordpress.com
Twitter: @stevestred
Instagram: @stevestred
Books: author.to/stevestred

www.ingramcontent.com/pod-product-compliance
Lightning Source LLC
Chambersburg PA
CBHW051413050726
47595CB00010B/4049